DRAGON'S OATH

DRAGON'S OATH

P. C. CAST and KRISTIN CAST

ST. MARTIN'S GRIFFIN

NEW YORK

DRAGON'S OATH. Copyright © 2011 by P. C. Cast and Kristin Cast. All rights reserved. Printed in the United States of America. For information, address St. Martin's Press, 175 Fifth Avenue, New York, N.Y. 10010.

Illustrations copyright © 2011 by Kim Doner.

www.stmartins.com

ISBN 978-1-250-00023-1

First Edition: July 2011

10 9 8 7 6 5 4 3 2 1

To all of our Warrior readers. We heart you!

As always, we'd like to acknowledge our agent and friend, Meredith Bernstein, without whom the House of Night would not exist.

Thank you to our wonderful St. Martin's Press family!

And a special thank-you to our friend, Kim Doner, who created the magickal art for this novella. It was a true pleasure to watch this story take form through her very talented pencil!

DRAGON'S OATH

CHAPTER ONE

Present-day Oklahoma

Anger and confusion stirred within Dragon Lankford. Was Neferet truly taking her leave of them so soon after the death of the boy and their goddess's cataclysmic visit?

"Neferet, what of the fledgling's body? Should we not continue to hold vigil?" With an effort, Dragon Lankford kept his voice calm and his tone even as he addressed his High Priestess.

Neferet turned her beautiful emerald eyes to him. She smiled smoothly. "You are right to remind me, Sword Master. Those of you who honored Jack with purple spirit candles, throw them on the pyre as you leave. The Sons of Erebus Warriors will hold vigil over the poor fledgling's body for the remainder of the night."

"As you wish, Priestess." Dragon bowed deeply to her, wondering why his skin felt so itchy—almost as if he was covered in dirt and grime. He had a sudden inexplicable desire to bathe in very, very hot water. *It is Neferet,* his conscience spoke softly to him. *She has not been right since Kalona broke free of the earth. You used to feel that . . .*

Dragon shook his head and set his jaw. Peripheral events did not matter. Feelings were no longer important. Duty was all encompassing—vengeance was utmost. *Focus! I must keep my mind on the job at hand!* he commanded himself, and then nodded quickly to specific Warriors. "Disperse the crowd!"

Neferet paused to speak to Lenobia before she departed from the center of the campus and headed in the direction of the professors' living quarters. Dragon barely spared her a look. Instead, his attention was pulled back to the fiery pyre and the boy's flaming body.

"The crowd is being dispersed, Sword Master. How many of us shall remain to watch by the pyre with you?" asked Christophe, one of his senior officers.

Dragon hesitated before he answered, taking a moment to center himself as well as to absorb the fact that the fledglings and professors who were milling uncertainly around the brightly burning pyre were obviously agitated and thoroughly upset. *Duty. When all else fails, turn to duty!*

"Have two of the guards escort the professors back to their quarters. The rest of you are to go with the fledglings. Be quite certain they all return to their rooms. Then stay close to the dormitories for the remainder of this terrible night." Dragon's voice was rough with emotion. "The students need to feel the protective presence of their Sons of Erebus Warriors so that they can, at least, be certain of their safety, even if it seems they can be certain of little else."

"But the child's pyre—"

"I will stay with Jack." Dragon spoke in a tone that allowed no interference. "I shall not leave the boy's side until the red glow of his embers turns to rust. Do your duty, Christophe; the House of Night needs you. I will see to the sadness that remains here."

Christophe bowed and then began calling out commands, following the Sword Master's orders with cold efficiency.

It seemed only seconds had passed when Dragon realized he was alone. There was the sound of the burning pyre—the deceptively soothing pop and crackle of the fire. Except for that, there was only the night and the vast emptiness in Dragon's heart.

The Sword Master stared into the flames as if he could discover the balm that would soothe his pain within them. The fire flickered amber and gold, rust and red, reminding Dragon of a delicate piece of jewelry—unique, exquisite, tied to a strand of velvet ribbon the color of fresh blood . . .

As if moving of its own accord, his hand went into his pocket. His fingers closed around the oval disk he found there. It was slim and smooth. He could feel only the faintest hint of the bluebird that once had been etched so clearly and beautifully on its face. The golden piece rested snugly in his hand. He cupped it, protected it, held it, before he slowly drew out his hand, the locket nestled within it. Dragon twined the velvet ribbon through his fingers, rubbing it with his thumb in a familiar, absentminded motion that spoke more of habit than thought. Expelling a deep breath that sounded more sob than sigh, he opened his palm and looked down.

The light from Jack's pyre flitted across the locket's golden surface. It caught the bluebird design.

"Missouri's state bird." Dragon spoke aloud. His voice was devoid of emotion, though the hand that held the locket shook. "I wonder if you can still be found wild, perching in the sunflowers that overlook the river. Or did your beauty and those of the flowers die out, too, along with everything else lovely and magickal in this world?" His hand closed on the locket, gripping it so tightly his knuckles turned white.

And then, as quickly as his fist had closed, Dragon released his hold on the locket, opening his hand and turning the gold oval over and over reverently. "Fool!" His voice was ragged. "You could have broken it!" Trembling fingers fumbled with the clasp, but when he finally unlatched it the golden piece opened easily, unharmed, to display the tiny etching that, although faded by time, still showed the smiling face of the petite vampyre whose gaze seemed to catch and hold his.

"How can you be gone?" Dragon murmured. One finger traced the old portrait on the right side of the locket, and then moved to the left half of the piece of jewelry to stroke the single blond curl that nestled there over the empty space where his youthful picture had once been. His gaze turned from the locket up to the night sky and he repeated the question louder, from his soul, crying out for an answer. "How can you be gone?"

As if in response Dragon heard echoing in the night air the distinctive croaking caw of a raven.

Anger rushed through Dragon, so hard and hot that his hands once again trembled—only this time he did not shake with pain and loss; he shook with the barely controlled need to strike out, to maim, to avenge.

"I will avenge her." Dragon's voice was like death. He looked down at the locket again and spoke to the shimmering blond curl it held. "Your dragon will avenge you. I will set to right what I allowed to go wrong. I will not make the same mistake again, my love, my own. The creature will not go unpunished. On that I pledge to you my oath."

A gust of wind, hot from the pyre, blew suddenly strong. It lifted the lock of hair and, while Dragon fumbled unsuccessfully to stop it, the curl floated out of his reach up, up, up on the heated draft, almost feather-like. It hovered there and then, with a sound much like a woman's gasp of surprise, the hot wind changed, inhaling, drawing the lock of hair down into the fiery pyre where it was turned to smoke and memory.

"No!" Dragon cried, falling to his knees with a sob. "And now I've lost the last of you. My fault . . . ," he said brokenly. "My fault, just as your death was my fault."

Through the tears that filled his eyes Dragon watched the smoke from his beloved mate's lock of hair whirl and dance before him—and then begin to shimmer magickally, changing from smoke to a dusting of green and yellow and brown sparkles that continued to curl around and around until they began to separate and form distinct parts of an image: the green sparkles became a long, thick stem—the yellow delicate petals of a flower with the brown circling within them to become its center.

Dragon wiped his eyes clear of tears, hardly able to believe what he was seeing. "A sunflower?" His lips felt as numb with shock as his brain. *It is her flower!* his mind shouted. *It must be a sign from her!* "Anastasia!" Dragon cried as numbness gave way to a terrible, wonderful wave of hope. "Are you here, my own?"

The image of the shimmering sunflower began to waver and change. The yellow flowed down in a cascade that became golden blond. The brown lightened to the color of sun-kissed skin, and the green melted down within the skin, swirling and morphing into shining orbs that became eyes that were turquoise and familiar and dear.

"Oh, goddess, Anastasia! It is you!" Dragon's voice broke as he reached out for her. But the image lifted–a glowing tease just beyond his fingertips. He cried out in frustration and then stifled the sound of his misery as his mate's voice began to spill around him like a musical stream over water-worn pebbles. Dragon held his breath and listed to the ghostly message.

I've bespelled this locket, for you: my own, my mate.
The day has come when death forced us to part.
You must know that for you, forever, I shall wait.
So until we meet again I hold your love safely within my heart.
Remember, your oath was to temper strength with mercy.
No matter how long apart we shall be, I hold you to that oath
     eternally . . . eternally . . .

The image smiled once at him before it lost its form and returned to smoke and then nothingness.

"My oath!" Dragon shouted, surging to his feet. "First Nyx and now you reminding me of it. Do you not understand that it is because of that cursed oath that you are dead? Had I chosen differently those many years ago, perhaps I could have kept all of this from happening. Strength tempered by mercy was a mistake. Do you not remember, my own? Do you not remember? I do. I will never forget . . ."

As Dragon Lankford, Sword Master of the House of Night,

held vigil over the body of a fallen fledgling, he stared into the burning pyre and let the flames take him back so that he could relive the pain and the pleasure—the tragedy and the triumph—of a past that had shaped such a heartbreaking future.

CHAPTER TWO

1830 England

"Father, you cannot disown me and banish me to the Americas. I am your son!" Bryan Lankford, third son to the Earl of Lankford, shook his head and stared disbelievingly at his father.

"You are my third son. I have four others, two older and two younger. None of them are as troublesome as are you. Their existence and your behavior make it quite simple for me to do this to you."

Bryan ignored the shock and panic his father's words threatened to break loose within him. He forced himself to relax–to slouch nonchalantly against the wooden door to the stall closest to him as he beamed the Bryan Lankford smile at the Earl, that disarmingly handsome grin that women found irresistible and made them want to seduce him, and men found charming and made them want to be like him.

The Earl's dark, unchanging expression said that he was well aware of the Bryan Lankford smile—and utterly unaffected by it.

"My decision is final, boy. Do not disgrace yourself further by unsuitable begging."

"Begging!" Bryan felt familiar anger stir. Why must his father always belittle him? He'd never begged for anything in his life—he certainly was not going to start now, no matter the consequences. "I do not beg you, Father. I simply am trying to reason with you."

"Reason? *Again* you cause an embarrassment for me because of your temper and your sword, and you ask me to reason with you?"

"Father, it was only a small altercation, and with a Scotsman! I did not even kill him. In actuality I wounded his vanity more than his body." Bryan attempted a chuckle, but the sound was cut off by the return of the cough that had been plaguing him all that day, only this time it was followed by a wave of weakness. He was so distracted by the betrayal of his body that he put up no resistance at all when his father suddenly closed the distance between them and with one hand fisted the cravat at Bryan's throat, ramming him against the wall of the stable with such force that the little breath left in his body whooshed from him. With his other hand the Earl knocked the still-bloody sword from Bryan's failing grip.

"You blustering little braggart! That Scotsman is a border

Laird. His lands adjoin mine, *which you know, as you are aware that his daughter and her bed are within a short day's ride of our estate!*" The Earl's face, flushed with anger, was so close to his son that his spittle rained over Bryan. "And now your impetuous actions have given this Laird all the proof he needs to go to our prattling fool of a new king and demand reparations for the loss of his daughter's maidenhead."

"Maidenhead!" Bryan managed to choke out. "Aileene's maidenhead was lost long before I found her."

"That is of no consequence!" The Earl tightened the strangle grip with which he held his son. "What is of consequence is that you were the dolt caught between her knees, and now that weakling king has all the excuse he needs to look the other way when thieving clansmen from the north sweep south looking for fat cattle to steal. Whose cattle do you think they will be after, son of mine?"

Bryan could only gasp for breath and shake his head.

With a look of utter contempt, the Earl of Lankford let loose his son, allowing him to fall, coughing violently, to the dirt floor of the stable. Then the nobleman motioned to the red-coated members of his personal guard who had been blandly watching his son's disgrace, singling out the pockmarked senior member of the squad. "Jeremy, as I already ordered, bind him like the miscreant he is. Choose two other men to accompany you. Take him to the port. Put him on the next ship to the Americas. I want never to see him

13

again. He is no longer my son." Then he motioned at the stableman. "Bring my horse. I have wasted enough of my precious time on this foolishness."

"Father! Wait, I—," Bryan began, but another coughing fit cut off his words.

The Earl paused only long to look down his long nose at his son. "As I already explained, you are expendable and now you are no longer my concern. Take him away!"

"You cannot send me away like his!" he cried. "How will I live?"

His father jerked his chin at Bryan's sword, which lay in the dirt not far from him. It had been a gift from the Earl when his precocious son had turned thirteen, and even in the dim, dusty light of the stable the jewels that encrusted the hilt glistened. "Perhaps that will be of more use to you in your new life than it was to me in your old one. Allow him to take the sword," he addressed the guards, "and nothing else, with him! Bring me back the ship's name and its captain's mark as proof that he has left England—have him gone before sunrise tomorrow and there will be a purse of silver waiting to split between you," the older man said, and then strode to his waiting horse.

Bryan Lankford tried to shout at his father—to tell him how sorry he would be later, when he remembered that though his third son was, indeed, his most troublesome, he was also his most talented, intelligent, and interesting—but another coughing fit gripped the seventeen-year-old so thoroughly that he could only gasp helplessly and watch his father's horse gallop off. He couldn't even fight as he wished he could when the Earl's guard bound him, then dragged him through the dirt of the stables.

"It's about time a little crowing cock like you was brought low. Let's see how you like being common." Laughing sarcastically, Jeremy, the oldest and most pompous of Bryan's father's guards, tossed him into the back of a poultry cart, before bending to pick up Bryan's sword and, with a calculating look at its glittering hilt, shove it through his own waistcloth.

By the time Bryan reached the port it was dark, both in the world around him and within his heart. Not only had his father disowned him and cast him from his family and out of England, but it was becoming more and more clear that he was in the grip of some horrible plague. How soon would it kill him? Before he was free of this stinking dock, or would he die after being dragged onto one of the merchant ships that bobbed in the black water of the bay?

"I'll no be taking a coughing chit like this aboard." The ship's captain held his torch higher, examining the bound and coughing boy. "No." He scowled and shook his head. "He'll no be crossin' the waters wit' me."

"This is the Earl of Lankford's son. You'll take him or answer to His Lordship about why not," growled the Earl's senior guard.

"I don't see no earl here. I see a shit-spattered boy who's got the ague." The seaman spit in the sand. "And I won't be answering to anyone, 'specially no nonexistent earl, if I be dead from this brat's sickness."

Bryan tried to stifle his coughing—not to reassure the captain, but to rest the burning within his chest. He was holding his breath when the man stepped from the shadows, tall, lean, and dressed all in black, his pale skin in stark contrast to the darkness that seemed to surround him. Bryan blinked, wondering if his feverish gaze was deceiving him—was that truly a crescent moon tattooed in the middle of his forehead surrounded by more tattooing? His vision was blurry, but Bryan was almost certain the tattoos looked like crossed rapiers. Then reason caught up with vision and Bryan felt a jolt of recognition. A crescent moon and the surrounding tattoo could mean only one thing: the man was no man at all—he was a vampyre!

It was then that the creature lifted his hand, palm facing outward directly at Bryan. The boy stared in wonder at the spiral that decorated that palm, and the vampyre spoke words that would forever alter his life.

"Bryan Lankford! Night has chosen thee; thy death will be thy birth. Night calls to thee; hearken to Her sweet voice. Your destiny awaits you at the House of Night!"

The creature's long finger pointed at Bryan and his forehead exploded in pain as he felt the tattooed outline of a crescent moon blaze brand-like into his skin.

His father's men reacted instantly. They dropped Bryan and moved away from him, staring in open horror back and forth between the boy and the vampyre. He noticed the ship's captain had left his torch to sputter in the sand and disappeared into the darkness of the pier.

Bryan didn't see or hear the vampyre approach—he only saw the guards moving nervously, grouping behind Jeremy, swords half drawn, indecision clear on their faces and in their actions. Vampyre warriors had awe-inspiring reputations. Their mercenary services were much sought after, but except for the beauty and strength of their women, and the fact that they worshiped a dark goddess, little was known by most humans of their society and inner workings. Bryan watched

Jeremy try to decide whether this creature, who was obviously what they called a Tracker, was also a dangerous vampyre Warrior. Then he felt an impossibly strong grip on his arm, and Bryan was lifted to his feet to stare up at the creature.

"Return to whence you came. This boy is now a Marked fledgling, and as such is no longer your responsibility." The vampyre spoke with a strange accent, drawing out his words almost languidly, which only added to the mystery and sense of danger he exuded.

The men hesitated, all looking to the senior guard, who spoke quickly, managing to sound arrogant and belligerent at the same time. "We need proof for his father that he has left England."

"Your needs do not interest me," the vampyre said solemnly. "Tell the boy's father that he boarded a ship tonight, though a much darker one than you humans planned. I have neither the time nor the patience to give you proof other than my word." Then he looked at Bryan. "Come with me. Your future awaits." With a swirl of his black cloak the vampyre turned and began striding away down the dock.

Jeremy waited until the creature had been swallowed by the darkness. Then he shrugged one shoulder and looked at Bryan with disgust, before saying, "Our mission is fulfilled. His Lordship said to put his brat of a son on a ship, and that is where he is going. Let us leave this fish-stinking place and return to our warm beds at Lankford Manor."

The men were turning away when Bryan drew himself up straight. He took just an instant to inhale a deep breath and savor the relief he felt when the choking, debilitating cough did not come. Then he stepped forward and spoke in a voice that was, once again, strong and steady. "You are to leave me my sword."

Jeremy paused and faced Bryan. Slowly, he pulled the sword from where he'd shoved it in his waistcloth. He ignored Bryan and instead studied the precious stone-encrusted hilt. His smile was calculating and his eyes were cold when he finally turned back to Bryan.

"Do you have any idea how many times your father called me from my warm bed to collect you from some brawl you'd gotten yourself into?"

"No, I do not," Bryan said flatly.

"Of course you do not. All you nobles care about is your own pleasure. So now that you've been disowned and are *not* nobility any longer I'll be keeping this sword, and the money selling it will gain me. Think of it as payment for what a pain in my arse you have been these past many years."

Bryan felt a rush of anger, and with it came a surge of heat throughout his body. Acting on instinct, the boy closed the distance between himself and the arrogant guard. In some

19

part of his brain Bryan knew his movements were preter-naturally swift, but he remained focused on the one thought that was a driving force within him: *The sword is mine—he has no right to it.*

With a motion that blurred, Bryan knocked the sword from Jeremy's hand and, in the same movement, caught it. As the other two guards moved forward, Bryan lunged low and stuck the point of the sword straight through the bones of the closest man's foot, causing the guard to double up and fall on the floor in agony. Bryan automatically rebounded and, chang-ing direction, flat-bladed the second guard across the side of his head, stunning him. Moving with a deadly grace, Bryan followed the motion of his sword, whirling around, and end-ing with the sharpened edge of the blade pressed firmly enough against Jeremy's neck that his skin beaded with drops of blood.

"This sword is mine. You have no right to it," Bryan heard his voice speaking his thoughts aloud, and was surprised by how normal he sounded—he wasn't even breathing hard. There was no way Jeremy or either of the other two fallen guards could know that everything inside him was burning with anger and outrage and the need for vengeance. "Now tell me why I should not slit your throat."

"Go ahead. Strike me. Your father is a viper, and even dis-owned you are his serpent of a son."

Bryan was going to kill him. He wanted to—his rage and his pride demanded it. And why shouldn't he kill him? The guard was only a peasant, and one who had insulted *him,* the son of an earl! But before Bryan could slice through the guard's neck, the vampyre's words sliced the air between them.

"I have no desire to be pursued and perhaps questioned by the British navy. Let him live. His fate, to return to serving those he despises, is far greater punishment than a quick death."

Still holding the point to the guard's neck, Bryan glanced behind him at the vampyre. The creature had spoken with a voice so calm it sounded almost bored, but his entire focus was on the guard's throat and the small drops of scarlet that Bryan's blade had freed. The vampyre's obvious desire intrigued as well as horrified the boy. *Is this what I am to become?*

Bryan shoved the guard from him. "He's right. Your life is better punishment than my blade. Go back to it and the bitterness with which you live it." Without another look at the man, Bryan turned his back on him and walked to the vampyre's side.

The vampyre inclined his head in a small nod of acknowledgment. "You made the correct choice."

"He insulted me. I should have killed him."

The vampyre cocked his head to the side, as if weighing the solution to a problem. "Did his calling you a snake insult you?"

"Well, yes. Calling me spoiled and trying to steal what is mine was also an insult."

The vampyre laughed softly. "It is no insult to be called a snake. They are creatures allied with our Goddess, though I do not believe he was just in naming you such. I watched as you bested those three men. You strike more like a dragon than a snake." While Bryan blinked in surprise he continued. "And dragons are above such petty insults as mere mortals might hurl at them."

"Are there dragons in America?" Bryan blurted the first of the jumbled thoughts that filled his mind.

The vampyre laughed again. "Have you not heard? America is filled with wonders." Then he made a sweeping motion with his hand, gesturing down the pier. "Come, let us go so that you may discover them. I have spent enough time on these archaic shores. My memories of England were not good, and nothing I have encountered during my wait for you has done anything to better them." The vampyre started off down the dock with Bryan almost jogging to keep up with his long strides.

"Did you say you have been awaiting me?"

"I did, and I have," he said, still moving purposefully down the dark pier.

"You knew about me?"

The vampyre nodded, causing his long brown hair to obscure his face. "I knew there was a fledging here I had to wait to Mark." He glanced at Bryan and his lips tilted up in a slight

22

smile. "You, young dragon, are the last fledgling I will ever Mark."

Bryan's brow furrowed. "Your last fledgling? What is happening to you?" He tried not to sound worried. After all, he barely knew this vampyre. And the creature was a *vampyre:* mysterious, dangerous, and strangely compelling.

The vampyre's slight smile widened. "I have finished my service as one of Nyx's Trackers, and am now able to return to my position as a Son of Erebus Warrior in the service of the Tower Grove House of Night."

"Tower Grove? That's in America?" Bryan's stomach tightened. He'd almost forgotten that his world had turned upside down in less than the space of one day.

"It is, indeed, in America. St. Louis, Missouri, to be exact." The vampyre had come to the end of the long pier—the darkest end, Bryan noted, as he could hear the creakings of a great ship and the lapping of water around it, but try as he might he couldn't see more than a hulking shadow bobbing on the water. He noticed the vampyre had stopped beside him and was studying him carefully. Bryan met his gaze squarely, though his body felt like a tightly coiled spring ready to come loose at any moment.

"I am called Shaw," the vampyre finally said, and held out his hand to Bryan.

"I am Bryan Lankford." Bryan paused and then managed

a smile that was only semi-sarcastic. "I am the *former* son of the Earl of Lankford, but you already know that."

When Shaw took Bryan's offered hand, he did so in the traditional vampyre greeting, grasping his forearm and not just his hand. Bryan mimicked his actions.

"Merry meet, Bryan Lankford," Shaw said. Then he let loose the boy's arm and made a gesture at the darkness and the ship that lay hidden within it. "This is the Ship of Night, which will bear me, and perhaps you as well, to America, and my beloved Tower Grove House of Night."

"Perhaps me as well? But I thought—"

Shaw held up a hand, silencing Bryan. "You must, indeed, join a House of Night, and quickly. That Mark," Shaw pointed at the outline of the sapphire crescent moon that still ached in the center of Bryan's forehead "means you must be in the company of adult vampyres until you either make the Change fully to vampyre, or . . ." Shaw hesitated.

"Or I die," Bryan said into the silence.

Shaw nodded solemnly. "Then you do know something of the world you are about to enter. Yes, young dragon, you will either complete the Change some time during the next four years, or you will die. This night you have begun a life path from which there is no turning back. Now, I told your father's guards that you would be joining me as I make the crossing to the New World because I saw that they were set on your departure from England, but the truth is more than your fate changed when you were Marked."

"For the better or for the worse?" Bryan asked.

"For exactly what you make of it yourself, Nyx be willing," he said cryptically, and then continued, "You cannot control whether you will successfully complete the Change, but you can control where you will spend the next several years. Should you wish to remain in England I can arrange for you to be taken to the London House of Night." The Tracker rested his hand briefly on Bryan's shoulder. "You no longer require your family's permission to pursue the future you most desire."

"Or I may choose to come with you?" Bryan asked.

"Yes, but before you make your choice I believe there is something you should see." Shaw turned to face the ship, which was visible to Bryan only as a huge, dark shadow resting ominously on the water, tethered by impossibly thick ropes. As if he had no trouble at all seeing through the thick blanket of the night, Shaw took two steps closer to the edge of the pier, and then he did something that utterly mystified Bryan. He turned so that he was facing south, raised his hands, and spoke four words softly: *"Come to me, fire."*

Instantly Bryan heard a crackling sound, and felt a surge of warmth in the air around him. Then he gasped as a ball of flickering fire swirled between Shaw's outstretched palms. The vampyre flung the fire, as if tossing a ball, at what Bryan could now see was a large standing torch, the oil-soaked top of which instantly took flame.

"Bloody hell!" Bryan couldn't contain his shock. "How did you do that?"

Shaw smiled. "Our Goddess has gifted me with more than the abilities of a Warrior, but that is not what I wanted you to see." Shaw lifted the torch and held it before them so that the proud prow of the huge ship, made of wood so dark Bryan thought it looked like it has been fashioned from night itself, was suddenly made visible. And then the boy blinked in surprise, as he realized exactly what he was seeing.

"It is a dragon," he said, staring at the carving of the masthead. It was truly spectacular—a black dragon, claws outstretched, teeth bared, ferociously ready to take on the world.

"It seemed to me, after the events of the night, to be a good omen," Shaw said.

Bryan stared at the dragon and was filled with the most intense flood of feelings he had ever experienced. It took him a moment to realize what they were, and then he knew: excitement and anticipation and longing all joined within him to create a single sense of purpose. He met the vampyre's gaze. "I choose to enter the dragon."

CHAPTER THREE

Tower Grove House of Night
St. Louis, 1833

"Merry meet, Anastasia! Please, do come in. It is a fortuitous coincidence that you are here. Diana and I were just discussing how happy we are to have such a young priestess of spells and rituals join the school as full professor, and I was going to call for you to tell you how pleased I am by how well you are fitting in here at Tower Grove."

"Merry meet, Pandeia, Diana," Anastasia said, fisting her right hand over her heart and bowing her head respectfully first to her High Priestess, Pandeia, and then to Diana, before she entered the large, beautifully appointed room.

"Oh, come now, you needn't be so formal with us when we are not in the company of fledglings," Diana, professor of vampyre sociology and the High Priestess's mate, spoke warmly to Anastasia as she stroked a very fat calico cat that spilled across her lap, purring loudly.

"Thank you," Anastasia said in a quiet voice that sounded older than her twenty-two years.

Diana smiled. "So, tell us, though you've only been here for a fortnight, are you becoming settled? Does it seem like home for you yet?"

Home, Anastasia thought automatically, *had never been filled with such beauty and such freedom.* She quickly shook the thoughts away and said politely and honestly, "It is not quite home yet, but I can feel that it will be. I do love the prairie and the lush gardens." Her gaze went to the fat calico and then to the gray tiger-striped male that had begun to wind around the High Priestess's legs. Then she blinked in surprise as she saw that both of the cats had six toes on each front paw. "Six toes? I've never seen such a thing."

Diana tugged at the calico's paw playfully. "Some say polydoctlys are aberrations of nature. I say they're just more advanced than 'normal' cats. A little like vampyres are more advanced than 'normal' humans."

"Oh, my! They look like mittens! I'm so hoping now that I've found my House of Night, a cat will choose me, too. It would be so wonderful if she had six toes!" Then Anastasia realized she was speaking her silly thoughts aloud and added hastily, "And, of course, I'm enjoying my students and my new classroom very much."

"It makes me happy to hear you say so," Pandeia said, laughing softly. "And there is nothing wrong with wishing for a cat, six-toed or otherwise. Young Anastasia, Diana and I were about to take our iced wine on the balcony. Please join us."

"I am grateful for your invitation," Anastasia said humbly, and reminding herself not to say anything silly, she followed the women and their cats as they opened the French doors and stepped out onto a lovely moonlight-bathed balcony on which sat white wicker chairs and a matching table that was laden with a crystal vase etched with a perfect crescent moon and filled with fragrant red roses, alongside a silver bucket brimming with ice and a carafe of wine the color of ripe cherries. Stemware etched with crescent moons that matched the gorgeous vase glistened in the silver light of the full moon.

Roses, ice, wine, and crystal. I'm accustomed to simplicity and rules, though both had been tempered with love. Will I ever get used to such luxuries? Anastasia pondered, feeling utterly uncomfortable as she sat in one of the chairs and tried not to smooth back her long blond hair or obsessively straighten her dress. And then she shot to her feet. "I–I should pour for you, Priestess," she said, smiling nervously up at the tall, statuesque, *mature* High Priestess.

Pandeia laughed and gently swatted her hand away from the carafe. "Anastasia, Daughter, please sit and compose yourself. I am a High Priestess, which means I am more than capable of pouring wine for myself and my guests."

Diana kissed her mate softly on the cheek before she took her own seat. "You, my darling, are more than capable of many, many things."

Anastasia saw the color in Pandeia's cheeks heighten ever

so slightly as the couple shared an intimate look. Anastasia's own cheeks warmed as she witnessed the exchange, and she looked quickly away. Though she'd spent the past six years immersed in House of Night society, first as a fledgling, then as a priestess in training, and now as a professor, she still sometimes found their open sexuality surprising. She'd often wondered what her mother would think of this female-empowered society. Would she accept it in the quiet, private way she had her daughter's Mark and Change? Or would it be too much for her—too shocking—and would she condemn it as the rest of their community would?

"Are we embarrassing you?" Diana asked, a smile in her voice.

Anastasia shifted her gaze quickly back to her High Priestess and her mate. "Oh, land sakes alive, no!" she blurted, and then felt her face flush fully hot, and knew it must be flaming red. She'd sounded just like her mother—and knowing that made her want to crawl under the table and disappear.

You are no longer a shy Quaker girl, Anastasia reminded herself firmly. *You are fully Changed vampyre, professor, and priestess.* She lifted her chin and attempted to look confident and mature.

Pandeia smiled kindly at her and raised one of the three crystal goblets she'd just filled. "I would like to propose a toast. To your success, Anastasia, and the completion of your first fortnight of teaching as our professor of spells and rituals. May you come to love Tower Grove House of Night as much as we love it." The High Priestess lifted her hand that wasn't holding the goblet of wine. She closed her eyes and Anastasia saw her lips moving silently, and then she made a scooping motion over the bouquet of roses, as if she was collecting their scent, before flicking her fingers at each of the three goblets. Anastasia watched in wonder as the wine in her glass swirled and then, just for an instant, within the swirling liquid there appeared the shape of a perfect rose blossom.

"Oh, goddess! The rose spirit—you made it appear in our wine," Anastasia blurted.

"Pandeia did not *make* the rose spirit appear. Spirit is her affinity. Our High Priestess made a loving request in celebration of you, young Anastasia, and the rose happily complied," Diana explained.

Anastasia exhaled a long breath. "All of this." She paused and her gaze took in the table, the two vampyres, their contented cats, and the exquisite estate that surrounded them. "It fills me with such feeling that it is as if my heart seems ready to burst from my chest!" Then she cringed in embarrassment. "Forgive me. I sound like a child. I just mean that I am grateful to be here—grateful that you chose me to join this House of Night as your professor."

"I shall share a secret with you, Anastasia. Pandeia's spirit affinity has made many vampyres who are much older and more experienced than you feel as if their hearts might burst,"

Diana said. "Only they were too jaded to admit it. I like your honesty. Don't lose it as you age."

"I will try not to," Anastasia said, and took a quick gulp of her wine as she tried to order her thoughts—to decide exactly how she would reveal to Pandeia and Diana the true reason she had come to them this night. Then she was sorry she'd gulped the wine. It was, of course, laced with blood, and the power of it sizzled throughout her body, heightening her nerves along with the rest of her senses.

"I, too, like your honesty," the High Priestess said to Anastasia between sips of her own wine, which seemed not to affect her at all. "It was one of the reasons we chose you to fill our professorial vacancy, even though you have only had two years of formal training in spells and rituals. You should know that you came very highly recommended from the Pennsylvania House of Night."

"My mentor was kind, Priestess," Anastasia said, setting her goblet back on the table.

"I also recall she said you are closely allied with the element earth," Pandeia said. "Which is another reason I felt you would be a good fit at our House of Night. This really is the gateway to the west. Here the mystery and majesty of the wonderful, untamed earth spreads in eager invitation before us—something I thought you would appreciate and find compelling."

"I do, but I do not claim to have an actual earth affinity," Anastasia explained. "I allow that I feel a strong connection to the land and, sometimes, when I am especially fortunate, the earth lends me some of her power."

Pandeia nodded and continued to sip her wine. "You do know that many priestesses do not discover they have a true affinity for one of the elements until they have served the Goddess for many decades. You may yet find that the earth has, indeed, been gifted to you with a full-fledged affinity; you are still very young, Anastasia."

"Please do not take offense at my question, but exactly what is your true age? You look barely old enough to have been Marked, let alone to have gone through the Change," Diana said, tempering her rather harsh question with a smile.

"Diana!" Pandeia's voice was gentle, but her look was tinged with disapproval as she frowned at her strikingly beautiful mate. "I did not invite Anastasia here to interrogate her."

"No, I do not mind the question, Priestess. Actually, I am becoming used to it," she said to Pandeia. Then she turned her gaze to Diana. Anastasia lifted her chin just a little. "I am twenty-two years old. My mentor priestess in Pennsylvania told me she believed me to be the youngest vampyre in America to be made a full professor. It is an honor I will try to live up to by being diligent and serious about my classroom and my students."

"Daughter, I have no doubt you are diligent and serious, but what I would like you to be is earthsome as well," Pandeia said.

"Earthsome? Forgive me, Priestess, I do not know that word."

"To be earthsome is to take on the characteristics of the earth. Be vibrant like a cluster of wildflowers, fertile like a field of wheat, sensual as an orchard of ripe peaches. Do not simply feel connected to the land; let it infuse you with its wonders."

"And remember that you are a vampyre priestess and professor. There is no need for you to dress like an oppressed human schoolmarm," Diana added.

"I—I do not want to appear frivolous," Anastasia admitted hesitantly, glancing down at the high-necked, unadorned bodice and straight, long skirt she'd worn—and loathed— since she'd joined the Tower Grove House of Night and begun teaching two weeks ago. "I am so close in age to my students that it is sometimes difficult for them to remember I am a professor."

Pandeia nodded in understanding. "But the simple truth is that you *are* close to the age of many of our fledglings. My advice is to make that a strength rather than something against which you battle."

"I agree," Diana said. "Use your youth as an asset instead of trying to hide it behind clothes any of your elders who have decent taste would never think of wearing–" She paused and gestured first at the flowing Grecian-styled gown she wore, and then at the high-waisted Spanish-style gauchos and the plunging neckline of the white lace blouse her mate wore.

"Anastasia, what Diana is trying to convey to you is that there is nothing wrong with being young," Pandeia picked up the thread of the conversation. "I am quite sure the female fledglings feel comfortable coming to you with concerns they would not have the courage to mention to any of the rest of us."

Anastasia sighed in relief, having been given the perfect opportunity to speak of what was foremost on her mind. "Yes, that has already proven true. It is, actually, why I sought you out this night."

Pandeia frowned. "Is there is a problem among the students I should be made aware of?"

"You mean one other than Jesse Biddle?" Diana said the name as if just speaking it left a bitter taste in her mouth.

"Biddle is a problem for all of us, vampyres and students alike, especially since the misguided humans of St. Louis made him their sheriff," Pandeia said. Then her gaze narrowed as she studied Anastasia. "Has he been harassing our fledglings?"

"No, not that I know of." Anastasia paused, and swallowed past the dryness in her throat, trying to order her thoughts so that her High Priestess would find value in her words. "The fledglings do not like Sherriff Biddle, but he is not the focus of their conversations. Someone else is, and in my opinion, he is creating quite a problem within the House of Night itself."

"Who has you so worried?"

"The fledgling they call Dragon Lankford," Anastasia said.

Both vampyres were silent for too many beats of Anastasia's heart. Then it appeared as if Diana tried to conceal a smile by taking a long drink of her wine while Pandeia cocked an eyebrow at Anastasia and said, "Dragon Lankford? But he has been away from Tower Grove competing in the Vampyre Games for the past two weeks. You and he have not even met, yet you say he is somehow creating a problem for you?"

"No, not for me. Well, yes, I suppose the problem does have to do with me, though it isn't technically mine." Anastasia rubbed her forehead. "Wait, I'll start again. You asked if there was a problem among the students I know of because I am close enough in age to the fledglings that they feel comfortable talking with me. My answer is yes, I do know of a problem, and it has been created by what I can only call an obsession with this fifth former the students call Dragon."

Diana didn't try to hide her smile any longer. "He is dynamic, and very popular, especially with the female fledglings."

Pandeia nodded in agreement. "Case in point—he just bested all of his opponents, fledgling and vampyre alike, to win the coveted title of Sword Master at the Vampyre Games. It is almost unheard of in our history for a fledgling to have won such a title."

"Yes, I know of his victory. It is all the girls could talk of today," Anastasia said wryly.

"And you see this as a problem? Dragon's swordsmanship is impressive already, and he has yet to have completed the Change," Diana said.

"Though it would not surprise me to see his adult tattoos appear very soon," Pandeia added. "I agree with Diana—there is nothing unusual about the girls being distracted by Dragon." The High Priestess smiled. "When you meet him you, too, may understand their distraction."

"It is not simple distraction that concerns me," Anastasia explained quickly. "It is the fact that as of close of school this night a total of fifteen fledglings, thirteen girls and two boys, have come to me, one at a time, begging me for love spells with which to ensnare Dragon Lankford."

Anastasia was relieved that this time the silence of the two women was filled with expressions of shock and surprise instead of amusement.

Finally Pandeia spoke. "This news is disappointing, but not tragically so. The fledglings are aware of my policy on love spells—they are foolish and can be dangerous. Love cannot be bespelled or coerced." The High Priestess shook her head, obviously annoyed at the fledglings. "Diana, I would like you to teach a lesson in the coming week on what happens when obsession is mistaken for love."

Diana nodded. "Perhaps I should begin with the story of Hercules and his obsession with the vampyre High Priestess Hippolyte, and the tragic end that brought about for both of them. It's a cautionary tale they should all know, but have obviously forgotten."

"An excellent idea." Pandeia turned her wide brown eyes on Anastasia. "I am assuming your response to these inappropriate requests has been to remind those mistaken fledglings that under no circumstances will you perform any type of love spell for them."

Anastasia drew a deep breath. "No, Priestess. That was not my response."

"Not your response! Why would you—," Diana began, but her mate's raised hand cut her off.

"Explain," was all the High Priestess said.

Anastasia met the vampyre's gaze unwaveringly. "I, too, have no use for love spells. Even when I was first Marked and began to show talent in spellwork my instinct told me love spells were dishonest. I am inexperienced but not naïve. I know love cannot exist with dishonesty."

"Insightful yet not an explanation," Pandeia said.

The young professor straightened her spine and shifted her gaze to Diana. "You called Lankford 'dynamic' and 'popular.' Did you not?"

"I did."

"Would you also say he is arrogant?"

Diana lifted one shoulder. "I suppose I would. But that is not unusual. Many of our most talented Warriors have a sense of arrogance about them."

"A *sense* of arrogance, yes. But is it not tempered with the experience and control of an adult vampyre?" Anastasia asked.

"Yes, it is," she agreed.

Anastasia nodded and then her gaze went back to her High Priestess. "There has been much talk of this Dragon. I have listened carefully. You are right when you say I do not know him, but what I have heard of him is that Dragon Lankford is a fledgling who relies on his sword and smile rather than his wisdom and wits. My instincts tell me that if my infatuated students saw this fledgling for who he really is, they would soon lose interest."

"What exactly did you tell the fledglings?" Pandeia asked.

"I told them I could not possibly break the rules of this House of Night and cast a love spell, but what I could do is create a drawing spell for each of them."

"There is a fine line between a drawing spell and a love spell," Diana said.

"Yes, and that line is created by clarity, honesty, and truth," Anastasia retorted.

"But I have a feeling each student who came to you was being clear and honest and truthful about wanting Dragon

Lankford's love," Pandeia said, looking disappointed in her young professor. "Therefore, casting a drawing spell on Dragon would work as a love spell. Semantics is the only thing that differs between the two."

"That would be true if a spell was cast on Dragon. My drawing spell will be cast on each of the students who came to me instead."

Pandeia's disappointment changed to a satisfied smile. "You intend the spell to make the fledglings see Dragon with more clarity."

"It will draw for each of them a vision of fledgling Lankford that is honest and truthful, and not tainted by childish infatuation with an inflated ego and a handsome smile."

"It could work," Diana said. "But the spell will take finesse and skill."

"My instinct tells me our young professor has both aplenty," Pandeia said.

"Gratitude for your confidence in me, Priestess!" Anastasia almost shouted in relief. Then she stood. "With your permission, I would like to cast the spell tonight, during the full moon."

Pandeia nodded in agreement. "It is the perfect time for endings. You have my permission, Daughter."

"It is my intent to end any unhealthy infatuations tonight," Anastasia said, fisting her hand over her heart and bowing to her High Priestess and her mate.

"You might not end all of the infatuations with Dragon to-night. Someone may still be drawn to all that arrogance and smiling, egotistical charm," Diana called after her.

"Then that person deserves exactly what she gets," Anastasia muttered.

CHAPTER FOUR

The spell began utterly, completely right. Later, Anastasia could only shake her head and wonder how anything that started so well could have ended so disastrously.

Perhaps it happened because she'd taken the time to change from the dreadfully confining clothes she'd mistakenly begun wearing since becoming a professor. After all, had she not been at that particular part in the spell, at that exact moment in that specific place—had one of those elements shifted just a heartbeat—everything would have changed.

Well, everything did change, just not as she'd intended.

The moonlight had felt so good, so right on her bare arms. That was one of the reasons she'd gone farther afield and closer to the mighty Mississippi River than she'd intended. The moon had seemed to be calling her forward, freeing her from the silly, self-imposed restraints she'd been placing on herself, in what was in retrospect a ridiculous attempt to be someone she was not.

Anastasia now wore the article of clothing she loved most: her favorite long, soft skirt the color of blue topaz. Just a month before being called to this new, wonderful House of Night, Anastasia had been inspired by a Leni-Lenape Indian maiden's dress. She'd sewn glass beads and shells and white leather fringe all around the skirt's hem and the low, rounded neckline of the sleeveless, butter-soft tunic top. Anastasia did a little twirling dance step, setting the shells and fringe in motion. *I will never wear those horrible, constricting clothes again. When I was a human that was all I was allowed to wear. I won't make that mistake again,* she told herself sternly, and then she flung back her head and spoke to the moon that hung heavy in the inky sky, "This is who I am! I am a vampyre professor, an expert in spells and rituals. And I am young and free!"

She was going to take her High Priestess's advice. Anastasia was going to be earthsome. She was going to find strength in her youth. "I am also going to dress as I wish, and not as if I'm an ancient schoolmarm." *Or a Pennsylvania Quaker like the human family I left behind six years ago when I was Marked,* she added silently. She would remember to keep the peaceful, loving part of her past without its confines and restraints. "I am earthsome!" she said joyfully, practically dancing though the calf-high grass that covered much of the prairie surrounding Tower Grove House of Night.

It wasn't just the physical freedom a change of clothes

allowed Anastasia—it was the sense of freedom Pandeia's confidence in her had provided that made all the difference. Add to that the fact that the night was warm and clear, and Anastasia was going to do something that brought her almost unspeakable joy: she was going to cast a spell that would actually benefit a House of Night—*her* House of Night.

But stopping in the field dotted with wild sunflowers had been a careless mistake. She knew sunflowers attracted love and lust, but Anastasia hadn't been thinking about love—she'd been thinking about the beauty of the night and the allure of the meadow. And the truth was she'd always loved sunflowers!

The meadow *was* breathtakingly lush. It was close enough to the Mississippi that Anastasia could see the willows and rowans that lined the high, bluff-like western bank. She couldn't actually see the river because of the trees and the bluff, but she could smell it—that rich scent that whispered of the earth's fertility and power and promise.

In the center of the meadow, perfectly situated to catch all of the silver light of the full moon, was a huge, flat sandstone boulder, just right for the altar she would need for her drawing spell.

Anastasia put her spellwork basket on the ground beside the large rock, and began setting out the ingredients for the ritual. First, she brought out the silver chalice her mentor had given her as a going-away present. It was simple but beautiful, adorned only with the etched outline of Nyx, arms raised cupping the crescent moon above her. Then Anastasia unwound the green, shimmery altar cloth from around the little corked jug filled with blood-spiked wine and flicked it open, letting it settle naturally across the top of the rock. She placed the chalice in the center of the rock, and then freed the big hunk of waxed paper from the basket, opening it to expose the loaf of fresh bread, the wedge of cheese, and the thick slices of fragrant, cooked bacon within. Smiling, she placed the paper and the food beside the chalice, which she took a moment to fill.

Satisfied with the scents and sights of the feast, which represented the bounty of the Goddess, she then withdrew five pillar candles from the basket. Anastasia found north easily by turning upriver, and it was at the northernmost part of the rock that she placed the green pillar, representing the element she felt closest to, earth. While she placed the rest of the candles in their corresponding directions: yellow for air in the east, red for fire in the south, blue for water in the west, and the purple spirit candle in the center, Anastasia controlled her breathing. She drew deep breaths, imagining pulling air infused with earth power up through the ground and into her body. She thought about her students and how very much she wanted the best for them, and how the best meant that they should see each other clearly and move forward in their paths with truth and honesty.

When the candles were set, Anastasia brought out the rest of the contents of the spellwork basket: a long braided length of sweetgrass, a tin that held wooden matches and a lighting strip, and three small velvet bags—one held dried bay leaves, another the spiky needles of a cedar tree, and the third was heavy with sea salt.

Anastasia closed her eyes and sent the same silent, heartfelt prayer to her Goddess that she did before every spell or ritual she'd ever attempted. *Nyx, you have my oath that I intend only good in the spell I work tonight.*

Anastasia opened her eyes and turned first to the east, lighting the yellow candle for air and calling the element to her circle in a clear voice, using simple words: "Air, please join my circle and strengthen my spell." Moving clockwise she lit all five candles, calling each element in turn, completing the spellwork circle by lighting the purple spirit candle in the center of the altar.

Then she faced north, drew another deep breath, and began to speak from her heart and soul.

"I begin with sweetgrass to cleanse this space." She paused to hold the end of the braid over the flame from the green earth candle. As it lit, she wafted it gracefully around her in a lazy loop, filling the air above the altar rock with thick smoke that rolled in waves. *"Any negative energy must leave without a trace."* She set aside the still-smoking braid and held her left hand out, palm cupped. Then she reached into the first of

the velvet bags. While she crumbled the dried leaves into her palm she continued the spell. *"Awareness and clarity come with these leaves of bay. Through earth I call their power today."* The cedar needles came next. Anastasia breathed in their fragrant scent as she mixed them with the crushed leaves in her palm, saying, *"Cedar, from you it is courage, protection, and self-control I seek. Lend me your strength so that my spell shall not be weak."*

From the final velvet bag she scooped out the tiny sea salt crystals, but instead of adding them to the other ingredients, Anastasia held up her palm, which was now filled with the bay/cedar mixture. She tilted back her head, loving that a warm, fire-kissed wind that smelled of river water lifted her thick fall of blond hair, giving evidence to the fact that the elements had, indeed, joined her circle and were there, waiting, to receive and fulfill her request. As she began to speak the words of the spell, Anastasia's voice took on a lovely singsong lilt so it sounded as if she was reciting a poem put to music only her soul could hear.

"A drawing spell is what I work tonight.
My wish is to cast clarity of sight.
With leaves of bay I will reveal the truth
Love should not be based on arrogant youth.
Cedar strength protects from the boy's misdeeds,
Lends courage and control to fulfill their needs."

The sea salt felt slick against Anastasia's fingers as she added the final ingredient to her spell. *"Salt is the key to bind this spell to me."* She moved over to the green candle, drew another breath, and ordered her thoughts. It was now that she needed to evoke Dragon Lankford's name and then speak each of the fifteen students' names in turn, sprinkling a pinch of what was now a magickally infused mixture into the earth flame, while she hoped and prayed each spell would stick and each student would see Dragon with clarity and truth and honesty.

"In this flame the magick cuts like a sword
drawing only the truth of Bryan Lankford!"

As she said his name it happened. Anastasia should have been sprinkling the first pinch of the mixture into the flame and speaking the name of the utterly Lankford-obsessed Doreen Ronney, and instead the night exploded around her in chaos and testosterone as a young fledgling burst from behind the nearest hawthorn tree, sword drawn.

"Move! You're in danger!" he shouted at Anastasia, giving her a rough shove. Off balance, her arms windmilled, so that the magickal mixture was tossed up, up, up, as she went down, down, down, landing roughly on her bottom. Which was where she sat, watching in openmouthed horror while the warm wind that had been present since she'd opened her spellwork circle caught the magickal mixture and gusted, dashing the entire palmful directly into the fledgling's face.

Time seemed to suspend. It was as if reality, for an instant, shifted and divided. One second Anastasia was looking up at the fledgling, frozen in the moment, sword up like the statue of a young warrior god. Then the air between her and the unmoving fledgling began to glow with a light that reminded her of the flame of a candle. It rippled and roiled, so bright that she had to lift a hand to shield her eyes. While she squinted against the glare, the brightness split down the middle, parting on either side of the fledgling as if framing his body in tangible light, and from the center of that, juxtaposed in front of the boy, Anastasia beheld another figure. At first he was indistinct. Then he took a step forward, toward her, so that the light illuminated him and he totally blocked her view of the fledgling.

He was the same general height and size as the boy. He, too, was brandishing a sword. Anastasia looked at his face. Her first thought, followed quickly by shock and surprise, was: *He has a kind face—handsome really.* And then she gasped, realizing what she was seeing. "You're him! The fledgling behind you. It's you!" Only it wasn't *really* the boy. That was clear. This new figure was a grown man, a full vampyre with the incredibly exotic-looking tattoos of two dragons, facing the filled-in crescent at the center of his forehead, bodies, wings, and tails stretching down his face to frame a firm jaw and full lips   lips that tilted up in a disarmingly charming smile at her. "No, you're not the fledgling," she said, looking from his lips up to his brown eyes, which were sparkling a reflection of his smile.

"You drew me, Anastasia. You should know who I am."

His voice was deep and pleasing to her.

"I drew you? But I . . . ," her voice trailed off. What had she said just before the fledgling appeared and managed to douse himself in her spellwork? Ah, she remembered! "I'd just said: 'In this flame the magick cuts like a sword drawing only the truth of Bryan Lankford!'" Anastasia cut off her own words, staring at the vampyre's tattoos . . . *dragon* tattoos. "How is this possible? You can't be Bryan Lankford! And how do you know my name?"

His smile widened. "You are so young. I'd forgotten." Holding her gaze with his, he swept her a courtly bow. "Anastasia, my own, my priestess, Bryan Lankford is exactly who you did draw. I am he." He chuckled briefly. "And I have not been called Bryan by anyone except you for a very, very long time."

"I didn't mean to *literally* draw you! And you're old!" she blurted, and then felt her face warming. "No, I don't mean *old* old. I mean you are older than a fledgling. You're a Changed vampyre. Not an *old* one, though." Anastasia wished desperately that she could disappear under the altar rock.

Bryan's laugh was warm and good-natured and very appealing. "You asked for the truth of me, and that is what you conjured. My own, this is who I will become in the future, which is why I am, as you say, *old* and a vampyre, fully Changed. That fledgling over there, behind me, is who I am today. Younger, yes, but also rash and entirely too sure of himself."

"Why do you know me? Why do you call me 'my own'?" *And why do you make my heart feel as if it is an excited bird that is ready to take flight?* she added silently to herself, unable to speak the words aloud.

He closed the small space between them and crouched beside her. Slowly, reverently, he touched her face. She couldn't really feel his hand, but her breath still caught at his nearness. "I know you because you are my own, as I am yours. Anastasia, look into my eyes. Tell me truthfully what you see."

She had to do as he asked. She had no choice. His gaze mesmerized her, as did everything about this vampyre. She stared into his eyes and became lost there in what she saw: the kindness and strength, integrity and humor, wisdom and love, utter and complete love. Within his eyes Anastasia recognized everything she'd ever imagined a man to be.

"I see a vampyre I could love," she said with no hesitation. And then hastily added, "But you're a Warrior, that's obvious, and I can't–"

"You see the vampyre you *do* love," he said. Stopping her words he leaned forward, cupped her face in his hand, and pressed his lips to hers.

Anastasia shouldn't have been able to feel anything. Later she replayed the scene over and over in her mind, trying to decide how a conjured phantom of a man could have possibly made her *feel* so much without actually being able to touch her at all. But then all she could do was tremble and hold her breath as desire for him, real or imagined, pulsed through her body.

"Ohhh," she breathed the word on a sigh when he moved slowly, regretfully away from her.

"My love, my own, I am a vampyre and a Warrior. I know it seems impossible right now, but I believe the truth is, to become the person you see—the man of kindness and strength, integrity and humor, wisdom and love—I need you. Without you, without *us,* I am only a shell of what I should be; I am the dragon without the man. Only you can make the man stronger than the dragon. Remember that when the young, rash, *arrogant* version of me attempts to drive you mad." He continued to back away from her.

"Don't go!"

His smile filled her heart. "I'm not going. I will never willingly leave you, my own. I'll be right here, growing and learning." He glanced behind himself at the frozen statue of a fledgling and chuckled, meeting her gaze again. "Even though that may be difficult for you to believe sometimes. Give us a chance, Anastasia. Be patient with me; we'll be worth it. Oh, and don't let me kill the bear. It wasn't going to harm you. It, like me, was only drawn to you because of a spell going slightly, magickally, awry. Neither he, nor I," he paused and his deep voice softened, "nor even my young, arrogant self, has anything malevolent in mind this night. And my own, my love, I will never allow anything to hurt you."

As he spoke those last words Anastasia felt a chill flow through her body as if some god or goddess had suddenly poured ice water into her veins. While she shivered with an odd mixture of foreboding and desire, the adult specter of Bryan Lankford, his gaze still locked with hers, surged backward. Light blazed as he was absorbed into the younger version of himself—who instantly began to move again.

Feeling like she had just been hit by the locomotive of one of those huge, coal-eating trains that traversed America, Anastasia watched the younger version of the vampyre, whose ethereal touch still thrilled through her body. He was wiping his tearing eyes with one hand, while with the other he brandished the sword at the enormous brown bear that appeared so suddenly before him on its hind legs. It was so large that Anastasia thought for an instant it, like the older version of Bryan Lankford, had somehow been conjured by her spellwork and was really mist and magick, smoke and shadows.

Just then the bear roared, making the very air around her vibrate, and Anastasia knew this was no illusion.

Lankford's eyes were clearing quickly, and he was moving with deadly intention toward the creature.

"Don't hurt it!" Anastasia shouted, "The bear was accidentally brought here by my spell—it has no malevolent intent."

Bryan stepped back, out of immediate range of the huge creature's claws. Anastasia watched him studying the bear. "Do you know this through your magick?" he asked without taking his eyes from the animal.

"I do! I give you my word on it," she said.

Bryan glanced quickly at her and Anastasia felt a strange jolt of recognition in that look. Then the fledgling blinked and said, "You had better be right."

Anastasia had to press her lips together to keep from shouting at him: *The grown-up version of you wouldn't have said that!*

She doubted he would have heard her shout. He'd already turned his entire attention back to the bear.

The big creature towered over the boy, but Bryan simply reached down, grabbed the candle nearest to him from the altar, and held it up before him. The flame of the red candle blazed like a torch. "Ha! Go!" he shouted in a voice that held more command than she would have expected from someone who wasn't even a vampyre. Yet. "Get out of here! Go on! This whole thing was an accident; the priestess didn't mean to draw you."

The bear flinched back from the brilliance of the candle, huffing and growling. Bryan moved a step forward. "I said go!"

With a huge sense of relief, Anastasia watched the beast

drop to all fours and, with one last huff at the fledgling, trot sedately away toward the river. Acting purely on instinct, she got to her feet and rushed toward Bryan.

"Okay, you're all right; you are safe, now. Everything is under control—," he was saying as she ignored him and took the still-flaming red candle from his hand.

"Don't break the circle. This spell has too much power to waste," she said sternly. She didn't look at him—she didn't want to be distracted. Instead Anastasia covered the flame with a protective hand and carefully placed the candle back in its place at the easternmost position on the altar, before she turned to face Bryan Lankford.

His hair was blond, long and thick and tied back, which made her remember the older Bryan's hair, which had also been the same light color, long and thick, but had fallen free around his shoulders, framing his kind face. Had it been just a little gray at his temples? Somehow she couldn't remember, though she could remember the exact color of his beautiful brown eyes.

"What is it? I didn't break your circle. The candle never went out. See, it's back right where it was before."

Anastasia realized she'd been staring at him without speaking. *He must think I'm completely daft.* She opened her mouth to say something that would explain a little of the strangeness of the night, and then she really looked at *him,* the young Bryan before her. He had salt scattered all over his face—crystals of it were caught in his eyebrows, and his hair was covered with bits of bay leaves and cedar needles. Her sudden giggle surprised them both.

His brows went up. "I risk my life to save you from a wild creature and you laugh at me?"

He was trying to sound stern and offended, but Anastasia could see the sparkle of humor in those brown eyes.

"You're wearing my spellwork, and, yes, that makes you look funny." It also made him look boyish and quite handsome, but she kept that part to herself. Or at least she thought she'd kept that part to herself. As the two of them stood there, staring at each other, the sparkle in Bryan's eyes seemed to become knowing. When his lips began tilting up, Anastasia's stomach gave a strange little lurch, and she quickly added, "Although I shouldn't laugh, no matter how funny you look. My spellwork all over you means I'm going to have to remake the entire mixture."

"Then you shouldn't have thrown it on me," he said with an arrogant flip of his head.

Anastasia's amusement began to fade. "I didn't throw it on you. The wind blew it into your face when I fell because you shoved me."

"Really?" He held up a finger, as if testing the direction of the breeze. "What wind?"

Anastasia's frown deepened. "It must have blown itself out, or maybe it has calmed because of the interruption of my spell."

"And I didn't *shove* you," he continued as if she hadn't spoken. "I moved you behind me so that I could protect you."

"I didn't need you to protect me. The bear was an accident. It was confused, not dangerous. I was casting a drawing spell, and somehow the bear got caught by it," she explained.

"So, it was a drawing spell." The irritation that had begun to creep into his voice vanished, to be replaced by an arrogant chuckle and another knowing look. "*That* is why you called my name. You want me."

CHAPTER FIVE

Dragon grinned as he watched the young priestess's face flush a lovely shade of pink.

"You have mistaken my intent," she said

"You said it yourself—you were casting a drawing spell. I heard you speak my name. Obviously, you were drawing me." He paused, thinking that it all made sense now. "No wonder I left Shaw and the rest of the Warriors and walked home by myself from the docks. I thought it was because of Biddle. He'd watched me before I left for the Vampyre Games, so I already knew he didn't like me, but tonight his stare was so hard, so strange, that I supposed it'd made me feel odd, almost as if I couldn't breathe, and I needed to be out here, where there was air and space and–" He broke off, laughing a little and giving her the beginnings of his famous smile. "But, no matter. The truth is I am here because you desire me." He rubbed his chin, considering. "We haven't met. I would re-member such beauty. Was it my reputation for prowess with the sword that has piqued your interest, or was it a more *personal* kind of prowess that–"

"Bryan, I don't desire *you*!"

"Call me Dragon," he said automatically, and then continued. "Of course you do. You just admitted your drawing spell. You need not be embarrassed. I'm flattered. Really."

"*Dragon*," she said in a way that he thought verged on sarcasm. "I am embarrassed, but not because *of* you. I'm embarrassed *for* you."

"You aren't making any sense." He wondered briefly if she'd hit her head when she'd fallen.

The priestess drew a deep breath and let it out in an exasperated sigh. Then she offered her hand and forearm to him, saying, "Merry meet, Bryan Dragon Lankford. I am Professor Anastasia, the new priestess of spells and rituals at the Tower Grove House of Night."

"Merry meet, Anastasia," he said, gripping her bare forearm, which was soft and warm to his touch.

"*Professor* Anastasia," she corrected him. Too soon, she released her grip on him and said, "You weren't meant to know about this spell."

"Because you don't want anyone to know you want me?" *Including me,* he added silently to himself.

"No. The spell has nothing to do with wanting you. It's the opposite, actually," she said. And then in a voice that sounded as if she was lecturing a classroom of fledglings, she continued "This is going to sound unkind, but the truth is I am here to cast what amounts to an anti–Dragon Lankford spell."

Her words took him aback. "Have I somehow done something to offend you? You do not even know me. How could you dislike me?"

"It isn't that I dislike you!" she said quickly, almost as if she was trying to cover something up. "Here is the truth of the matter: in the fortnight I have been teaching at Tower Grove House of Night fifteen fledglings have come to me to ask for love spells with which to bespell you."

Dragon's eyes widened. "Fifteen? Really?" He paused and took a quick mental count. "I can only think of ten girls who would want to bespell me."

The professor didn't look at all amused. "I would say you underestimate yourself, but I do not think that is possible. So I'll just assume you are better at swordplay than addition. Be that as it may, I came out here tonight intending to cast a spell that would draw to each of your besotted admirers the truth of you so that they could see clearly and honestly that you aren't the right mate for them, which would end their silly infatuations," she finished in a rush.

He couldn't remember the last time he had been so surprised. No, that wasn't true. The last time he'd felt this kind of soul-deep surprise was when the night had been illuminated to reveal the masthead of a ship and a new life. He shook his head and said the first thing that came to mind. "This is hard for me to believe. You really dislike me. Women usually like me. Quite a lot, actually."

"Obviously. That is why thirteen of them asked for me to bespell you."

He frowned. "I thought you said fifteen before."

"Thirteen girls. Two boys," she said dryly. "Apparently boys like you quite a lot, too."

Unexpectedly, Dragon laughed. "There you have it! Everyone likes me, except you."

"What I do not like is the thought that so many impressionable young fledglings are infatuated with you. It's simply not healthy."

"Not healthy for whom? I feel just fine." He smiled at her then, turning on every bit of his charm.

Dragon thought he saw her stern look relax a little and those big turquoise eyes soften, but her next words dashed cold water all over him.

"If you were more mature you would care about others' feelings."

He scowled. "Really? I'm almost twenty." Dragon paused and looked her up and down appraisingly. "How old are you?"

"Twenty-two," she said, lifting her chin.

"Twenty-two! That's too young to be a professor *and* too young to be lecturing me on being more mature."

"And yet I *am* your professor of spells and rituals, and someone should lecture you about what you would be if you acted older. Who knows, with a little guidance you might grow up and be a Warrior of integrity and honor."

"I have just returned from games where I earned the title of Sword Master. I already have integrity and honor, even though I'm not yet a fully Changed vampyre."

"You can't win integrity and honor from *games*. You can only earn them from living a life dedicated to those ideals." Her eyes held his and he realized that she wasn't speaking to him with condescension. She sounded oddly sad—almost defeated. And Dragon had no idea why that made him suddenly want to say something—do something, anything that would make the little furrow of worry on her otherwise smooth brow disappear.

"I know that, Anastasia—Professor Anastasia," he corrected himself this time. "I am already dedicated to my Sons of Erebus training. I will be a Warrior someday, and I will uphold their standards of honesty and loyalty and valor."

He was pleased to see her smile, though it was slight. "I hope you do. I think you could make an extraordinary Warrior someday."

"I'm already extraordinary," Dragon said, his smile back.

And then she surprised him again by looking him squarely in his eyes, almost as if she was a Warrior herself, and saying, "If you're so extraordinary, then prove it."

Dragon brandished his sword and bowed to her, hand fisted around the hilt, pressing it to his chest just as if he was a full Son of Erebus Warrior and she his priestess. "Send me on a task! Point me at the bear I must slay to prove myself worthy."

This time her smile was full, and Dragon thought it lit up her already beautiful face with a happiness that seemed to glow around her. Her mouth, with its full lips tilted up, was distracting him so that he had to blink in confusion and say, "What? Me?" when he realized she was pointing directly at him. "Even a vampyre who is too young to be a professor should be able to see that I am not a bear."

"I was assuming you were speaking metaphorically when you asked me to set you on a quest to prove your worth."

"Quest?" He blinked. He'd just been kidding. What was she thinking?

"Well, I suppose it doesn't really qualify as a full quest, but it is a way you can prove to me that you're extraordinary."

He took a swaggering step toward her. Now this was more like it! "I am ready to do your bidding, my lady," he said in his most charming voice.

"Excellent. Then come over here to my altar. You are going to help me cast this spell."

His swagger ended. "You want me to help you with a spell that will make girls dislike me?"

"Do not forget the two boys. And the spell won't make them dislike you. It will make them see you more clearly because it will get rid of their haze of infatuation for you."

"I have to tell you, this sounds a little dodgy to me. It seems a lot like cutting my arm off to prove that I'm an extraordinary swordsman."

"You do not have to help me." She turned back to the altar, fussing with the element candles and then the three little velvet bags that sat beside the chalice and food.

Dragon shrugged and started to walk away. It was no matter to him that this odd young priestess was set on making his love life difficult. So what if thirteen fledglings were no longer interested in him? (He didn't count the guys.) One thing he'd learned since he'd first discovered the pleasures of women was that there were *always* women who wanted him. He had even started to chuckle to himself when her next words drifted across the distance between them.

"Actually, pay no mind to my request. You should be getting back to the House of Night. Dawn approaches. Most fledglings are already in their beds."

He stopped and whirled around, wanting to spit fire at her. She'd spoken to him as if he was a child! But she didn't realize how her words had affected him. Anastasia was still puttering around the altar, her back to him, as if she had already completely erased Dragon Lankford from her mind.

She was wrong about him. He wasn't a child and he didn't lack honesty or loyalty or valor. He'd show her by . . . by . . .

And then he heard himself saying, "I'll stay and help you with the spell."

She looked over her shoulder at him and he saw surprise and something else, something that might have been pleasure and warmth in those big blue eyes. But her voice was nonchalant. "Good. Come over here and sit there, on the edge of the rock." She pointed. "Be careful not to disturb the altar cloth or knock over a candle."

"Yes, my lady. Anything you say, my lady," he muttered.

As he rejoined her she raised a brow at him but didn't say anything and went back to arranging the candle and neatening the altar.

Dragon studied her while she worked. His first impression of her held—she was a beauty: petite with long, wheat-colored hair that fell straight and thick to her waist. But even though she was small, she still had generous curves, which he could easily see through her sheer linen top and flowing blue skirt. He didn't usually pay much attention to what women wore— he preferred his women naked—but Anastasia's clothing was decorated with shells and beads and fringe, making her look fey and Otherworldly, an effect that was enhanced by her tattoos, which were graceful vines and flowers, so exquisite in detail they looked real.

"All right. I'm ready to begin again. Are you?" she asked.

He blinked and shifted his attention to the altar, not liking that she'd caught him staring. "I'm ready. Actually, I'm looking forward to hearing the names of the fledglings who asked for love spells." He turned his gaze from the altar to meet hers, being sure he put a challenge in his voice.

Anastasia's look remained unruffled. "Because you are aiding me with the spell, I won't need to call the fledglings' names. Your presence and cooperation add enough strength to my casting that it will affect anyone who has been distracted by you."

Dragon exhaled with a snort. "It sounds like it's a good thing I don't have a ladylove at this moment. What we're about to do would certainly mess that up."

"No, it wouldn't. Not if that person was truly interested in *you* and not some overblown image of you."

"You make me sound like an arrogant ass," he said.

"Are you?"

"No! I'm just me."

"Then this spell will not affect anyone who wants *just you*."

"All right, all right. I understand. Let's get this over with. What do you want me to do?"

She answered with a question of her own. "You have taken three years of spells and rituals classes, haven't you?"

He nodded. "I have."

"Good, well, I'll mix the spellwork herbs in your hand. Hold it up like a cup." She demonstrated with her own. "Like this. The herbs touching you will help lend strength to the

71

spell. Do you think you could manage the completion of at least some of the parts of the actual spellwork if I lead you through it?"

He stifled his irritation. She didn't sound patronizing. She sounded as if she hadn't actually considered the possibility that he might enjoy class—might be good at anything besides swordplay.

Professor Anastasia was in for a surprise.

"If you have to ask, you must not have checked out my class work record from the previous spells and rituals professor," he said blandly, hoping that his tone would make her believe she would have found one substandard grade after another.

The young professor sighed heavily. "No, I did not."

"So all you really know about me is how infatuated some of the other fledglings are with me."

Her eyes met his and, again, he saw an emotion he couldn't identify in their cornflower depths. "I know that someday you will be a Warrior, but that does not mean you can cast a spell."

"All I can do is to give you my word I will do my best tonight," he said, wondering why it mattered at all to him what she thought.

Anastasia paused, as if she was choosing her response carefully. When she finally spoke it was just to say a simple, "Thank you, Bryan." And she bowed her head slightly, respectfully, to him.

"Call me Dragon," he said, trying not to show how much that one small sign of respect had affected him.

"Dragon," she repeated. "I'm sorry. I keep forgetting. It's just that 'Bryan' seems to suit you."

"You would know that 'Dragon' suits me were you on the other side of my sword," he said. And then realizing how arrogant that must have sounded he added hastily, "Not that I would ever attack a priestess. I just meant that if you saw me during a swordfight you would understand my nickname. When I fight I become the dragon."

"That probably won't happen any time soon," she said.

"You truly dislike me."

"No! It has nothing to do with you. I dislike violence. I was raised—" Anastasia broke off, shaking her head. "*That* has nothing to do with the drawing spell, and we need to keep focused. Let's begin. Take three deep, slow breaths with me and clear your mind, please."

Dragon didn't want to. He wanted to ask her about how she'd been raised—about what had happened to her that had made her dislike violence so much—but the three years of spells and rituals training had him automatically following her lead and breathing along with her.

"The circle is already cast; we won't need to redo that," she said, taking a thick braid of half-burned grass from the altar. Anastasia glanced at him. "Do you know what this is?"

"Sweetgrass," he said.

"Good," she said. "Do you know what it's used for in spell-work?"

He made himself hesitate, as if he had to think hard to remember the answer. "Clearing negative energy?" Bryan purposefully made the answer into a question.

"Yes. That's correct. Very good." Anastasia spoke to him like he was a first-year fledgling. He hid his smile from her while she held the braided grass over the green earth candle. It relit easily. Then, wafting it clockwise around them, she turned to him and said, *"I begin with sweetgrass to cleanse this space . . ."* She paused, giving him an expectant look.

"Any negative energy must leave this place." With no hesitation, he said the rest of the opening spellwork line that completed the sweetgrass cleansing.

She beamed her pleasure in a sweet smile that made his breath catch in his throat, and Dragon was suddenly very, very glad he'd always been especially good at spells and rituals.

Anastasia placed the smoking braid back on the altar and then she took a pinch of herbs from the first velvet bag. She walked to him and he held his hand up for her, palm cupped, as she'd shown him. Anastasia sprinkled the bits of dried leaves, whose smell was familiar to him not just because he'd recently had the things blown in his face but also because he actually had spent the past three years paying attention in class. So when the priestess said, *"Awareness and clarity come with these leaves of bay . . . ,"* paused, and glanced at him it was an automatic, easy response for him to complete the line with, *"Through earth we call their power today."*

She rewarded him with another sweet smile before going to the second velvet bag. She returned to sprinkle dried needles over the bay leaves. *"Cedar, from you it is courage, protection, and self-control I seek."*

"Lend us your strength so that this spell shall not be weak," he recited quickly, not waiting for her pause.

This time Anastasia's smile seemed thoughtful, which made Dragon feel self-satisfied. More than a little smug, he was sitting there, smiling, knowing that the last ingredient of the spell would be salt to bind it, when the priestess shocked him completely by reaching forward and resting her hand softly on his head. He felt a jolt at her touch and his gaze went to hers. Her eyes widened and her voice definitely sounded breathless as she said, *"A part of this spell should come from you . . ."*

She paused and this time all he could do was sit there, silent, with his pulse pounding as her hand slid down toward his cheek. *"So that it is cast straight, strong, and true."* Her slim white fingers wrapped around several strands of hair that had escaped from the piece of leather that held the rest of it back, out of his way. Then she tugged. Hard. And plucked several strands from his head, which she dropped into his waiting palm.

Dragon resisted the urge to yelp and rub his scalp.

Only then did she turn to the third velvet pouch and come back with the crystals of salt, but she didn't sprinkle them over the mixture in his hand. Instead she took his other hand and led him from where he was sitting on the altar rock. Slowly, as she still held his hand in hers, the two of them began to walk clockwise around the glowing candles. Anastasia's voice changed as she got to the heart of the spell. Dragon couldn't complete the lines for her because he'd never heard this particular casting, but as she spoke and they moved around the stone he could feel the power of the spell wash over them. He became caught in her words, drawn to them as if they had texture and touch.

"A drawing spell is what we work tonight.
Our wish is to cast clarity of sight.
With leaves of bay we will reveal the truth
Love should not be based on arrogant youth.
Cedar strength protects from the boy's misdeeds,
Lends courage and control to fulfill their needs."

Dragon was so caught up in the sound of her voice that it took him a moment to process what she was actually saying.

By the time he understood she was probably calling him an arrogant miscreant, they'd come to a halt before the red fire candle and she turned to face him. Cradling his hand that cupped the herbs, she added the salt to the mixture, intoning, *"Salt is the key to bind this spell to me."*

Then she guided their joined hands over the red candle and, as she scooped out the mixture and fed it to the flame, said, *"In this flame the magick cuts like a sword drawing only the truth of Bryan Dragon Lankford!"*

With a *whoosh!* the flame ate the mixture, blazing up so high that Dragon had to pull his hand back to avoid being scorched.

At the Tower Grove House of Night, fifteen young fledglings paused. It was near enough to dawn that seven of them were already asleep, and in their dreams drifted a suggestion, scented with bay and cedar.

This then is true:
Dragon Lankford's future will not touch you . . .

Sally McKenzie was giggling with her roommate, Isis, and talking about how handsome Dragon was when suddenly she cocked her head and told Isis, "I—I think we should change our minds.

"He is brave—he is strong—
but for both of us Dragon Lankford is wrong."

Isis, her giggles stilled, shrugged and nodded in agreement. Both girls blew out their bedside lights and went to sleep feeling more than slightly uneasy.

Into the two infatuated boys' minds came the clear thought:

You will never know Dragon Lankford's touch;
his desires are not as such.

One fledgling wept quietly into his pillow. The other stared at the full moon and wondered if he would ever be loved.

* * *

Four of the six fledglings who were finishing their turn at kitchen duty hesitated at their work. Camellia looked at Anna, Anya, and Beatrice and said:

"I am too smart
to believe Dragon would ever give me his heart."

Anna gasped and dropped the porcelain cup she was holding. It shattered into the stunned silence.

"I would believe I found love in his bed,
but he would use and discard me instead."

Then Anya spoke, bending to help Anna clean up the shattered cup:

"His sword is his life;
I care not for such strife."

Next, Beatrice's face lost all of its color as she whispered:

"A human consort is my fate.
With a vampyre I will never find my true mate."

* * *

In the sumptuous living quarters of the Tower Grove House of Night's High Priestess, Pandeia was welcoming her mate into their bed when Diana's beautiful face registered surprise and she said:

"The Lankford fledgling's fate will be
beyond what you or I could possibly see."

"Diana? Are you well?" Pandeia touched her mate's cheek and looked deep within her eyes.

Diana shook her head like a cat ridding itself of water. "I am. I–that was odd. Those words were not mine."

"What were you thinking of before you spoke?"

She shrugged. "I suppose I was wondering if all the Warriors had returned from the games yet, and was thinking that Dragon has done our House proud."

The High Priestess nodded, suddenly understanding. "It is Anastasia's spell. It has drawn the truth about Dragon to those who were thinking of him at its casting."

Diana snorted. "I am hardly a besotted fledgling."

Pandeia smiled. "Of course you are not, my love. This demonstrates the strength of young Anastasia's spell. We can rest assured there will be no obsessed fledglings trailing about after him tomorrow."

"I almost feel sorry for the boy."

"Do not. If any of the fledglings were meant to love him, a splash of reality wouldn't wash true love away. And anyway, what was revealed to you shows that Dragon does, indeed, have a bright future."

Diana returned her mate's embrace, saying, "Or, at the very least, he'll have an interesting one."

At the Chicago House of Night, where the Vampyre Games had recently concluded, Aurora, a beautiful young vampyre, paused mid-word in the letter she was composing to the fledgling who had warmed her bed and her heart after he had defeated every swordsman who came against him. Dragon Lankford had claimed the title of Sword Master, along with Aurora's affection. Yet now she found herself putting aside her quill and lifting the thin paper sheet to touch the flame of the closest candle to her as she realized the truthfulness of the words that flitted through her mind whispering:

It was but a fling.
Another vampyre will truly make my heart sing.

What had she been thinking? Dragon had been a lovely diversion and no more.

* * *

And, finally, inside the forbidding brick building that served as jailhouse for St. Louis, Missouri, the whispers on the wind drifted down . . . down . . . down . . . to the bowels of the place and the hidden room in which Sherriff Jesse Biddle paced back and forth in front of the creature he held his captive in a cage of silver. He didn't actually talk *to* it so much as talk *at* it. "I have to learn how to use more of your power. I need to be able to stand against the vampyres. They're too blatant. It's like they think they're normal—that they have a right to be here!" he shouted. "I hate 'em. I hate 'em all! Especially that snot-nosed brat of a fledgling. You shoulda seen him get off the boat tonight. All big chested with his victory. Do you know what he calls himself? *Dragon* Lankford! He ain't no dragon. He's the same little bastard who's been struttin' round here for three years with that bright, shiny sword actin' like he's better then everyone—every *human*. What an arrogant little son-of-a—"

The keening from the creature was eerie. It made Biddle's skin crawl.

"Shut up or I'll throw some of that salt water on you again. That'll burn you up good like the proper chicken you are!"

Eyes that looked disturbingly human in the face of the enormous raven met his. Though the creature was only semi-substantial, its eyes glowed a strong, steady red.

"Through your obsessssion with Dragon Lankford hissss
    future I ssssee.
He will change hisssstory."

Biddle looked at the thing with disgust. "Why would I
care about that?"

"His love issss the key
to defeat the likessss of you and me."

"What are you talking 'bout, foul beast?"

"If Dragon is allowed to burn bright
he will extinguish the Dark light."

That caused Biddle to pause. He'd trapped this semi-
substantial manbeast as it absorbed the last bits of strength
from a dying Indian Shaman. The old redskin had managed
to throw this strange cage of silver around the creature, but
the Shaman had been too weak—too near death—to recover
from the creature's attack when Biddle had happened by the
old man's shack. The old man's last words had been: "Burn
sweetgrass to ward it off. Weight the cage with turquoise stones.
Throw it in a barrel of salt water so that it can never take another's power . . ."

Biddle had quickly decided he'd be damned if he'd waste

his time following an old, dead Injun's orders. He started to go, leaving the body and the thing in the cage for the next passerby to clean up.

Then the creature had turned its red eyes on him.

Human eyes.

Almost as repulsed as he was fascinated, Biddle had moved closer to try to see exactly what the thing was.

It was then that Biddle saw them. The moving darkness within the shadows surrounding the thing.

He'd come closer to the cage.

It was then that Biddle felt it. The power that slithered from the creature, through the cage, and along the floor to the dead man, and there it paused and hovered and then descended into the blood that had pooled on the ground around his mouth.

Something about that wriggling, shadowy darkness had goaded Biddle to move, to get closer, to touch. Acting on an impulse from the basest part of his mind, Biddle stepped between the cage and the dead man, wading into the strands of darkness.

Remembering, Sherriff Biddle closed his eyes in ecstasy. The pain had been cold and sharp and immediate, but so had been the power and pleasure that had swelled though him as some of the darkness had been absorbed through his skin and into his soul.

Biddle hadn't destroyed the creature.

He'd kept it trapped and fed it blood, but only occasionally. Because what if by feeding the thing got stronger—just like Biddle did. What if it managed to break through the cage of silver?

And now Biddle stared at the semi-formed creature of shadow and tried to convince himself he was not held as captive as his prey.

Then the thing, moving restlessly, spoke in a strange singsong with more animation than it had shown in the fortnight he'd had it, repeating:

"Hear the truth this night:
If Dragon is allowed to burn bright
he will extinguish the Dark light."

Biddle moved closer to the cage. "The Dark light. You mean the stuff you're made of—the stuff that surrounds you." *The stuff I can sometimes siphon from you,* he thought but didn't say.

The creature's red gaze met his, and Biddle knew it hadn't mattered whether he'd said it aloud. The thing knew.

"Yesss, to keep the power you desire
you must kill his love, the Anastasia vampyre."

Dragon was still blinking bright dots of flame away from his vision when he smiled at Anastasia and said, "Your spell seems to have worked."

"*Our* spell," she said softly, and gifted him with another smile. "Our spell was strong." Anastasia paused and then asked, "Would you close the circle with me?"

A rush of unexpected pleasure had him not trusting his voice, so Dragon only nodded.

"Good, I'm glad. It's only right that we close it together." Anastasia tilted her head back and said, "Thank you, spirit, for joining our circle tonight." Then she leaned down and blew out the purple candle.

Dragon went to the green candle, cleared the thickness from his throat, and said, "Thank you, earth, for joining our circle tonight." He blew out the flame.

In turn, together, they thanked water, fire, and air. Then the young professor faced him, took both of his hands in hers, and said, "Thank you, Bryan Dragon Lankford, for joining my circle tonight."

It was at that moment that Bryan Dragon Lankford realized that Anastasia wasn't just a beautiful vampyre and a gifted priestess. She was the *most beautiful* vampyre and *most amazing* priestess he'd ever seen. And without thinking, he bent and kissed her smiling lips.

CHAPTER SIX

His kiss was so unexpected that Anastasia was surprised into complete stillness. She just stood there, holding his hands, while he pressed his lips to hers.

Had she realized he was going to kiss her she would have moved away.

But she hadn't realized, so she didn't move.

And then the oddest thing happened. His touch was nothing like she'd imagined. He should have been too forceful or too awkward or too demanding. He wasn't. He was sweet and strong and just hesitant enough that she knew he, too, had been taken by surprise by the kiss.

Still, Anastasia was going to pull away. She should have pulled away. And she would have, had she not remembered the fully Changed vampyre with the kind, trustworthy eyes and the boyishly charming smile, and a kiss that was very, very similar—only this one she could truly feel. *My own . . .* he'd called her *my own* and her heart had responded before her mind could think to, which was exactly what was happening at that moment. Her body was responding to Bryan's touch before her mind could think to stop it. So she leaned into him, and kissed him gently and completely back.

While her mind wasn't thinking and her body was busy feeling, something bitterly cold brushed the back of Anastasia's skirt and lifted her hair, causing real life to intrude upon their kiss. Confused about the strange sensations coming from behind her, Anastasia was just starting to pull away from Bryan when the sound of wings exploded from behind them.

The sound terrified her like nothing before.

Pure fear pulsed through her. Anastasia stared wildly up at Bryan. "Something terrible is coming!" she gasped.

The change that came over him was instant. He went from dreamy-eyed, gentle fledgling to a Warrior—sword drawn and body tense.

"Stay here, next to the boulder and behind me." This time he didn't shove her off her feet. Instead he led her quickly into a defensive position and then turned to face whatever was lurking in the predawn.

Heart pounding, Anastasia crouched behind him, peering out at the grayish gloaming. Filled with foreboding, she waited for *it* to attack.

Nothing moved.

No malevolent creature of nightmare fell down upon them. No marauders swarmed. Nothing bad happened at all. All around them was only the meadow and the distant scent of the river.

She saw his broad shoulders begin to relax and readied herself for his discounting comment. When he turned to her, Anastasia saw only an alert concern in his expression.

"Do you know what it was?" he asked.

"No." She ran a shaky hand through her hair. "But I give you my word I wasn't pretending."

"I know that," he said. "A Sword Master is not just good with a blade. He's good with reading bodies and judging reactions. You were fearful." He reached out, took her hand, and helped her to her feet. Their hands lingered together for a moment. He squeezed hers before he let it go, and then Bryan reached for the chalice that sat full and ready in the middle of the altar. "Drink this and eat some of the food. It'll help. Plus, you should ground yourself after such a powerful spell."

As she sipped the fortifying wine and nibbled on the bread and cheese, Bryan disassembled the altar quickly, while he kept watch around them.

"Did you feel it? The cold?" she asked.

"No."

"Did you hear the wings?"

"No." He met her gaze. "But I believe you felt it and heard it."

"Some Indian tribes believe birds carry bad omens. Especially black birds," she said.

"I like to believe Nyx wants us to make our own omens," he said. Then he smiled and pointed at a clump of wildflowers not far from them and the brilliant blue bird with a splash of orange on its chest that fluttered there. "That is definitely not a bad omen."

Anastasia found her smile again. "No, it's a beautiful bird."

"And it's on those enormous yellow flowers. That has to be good, too."

"They're sunflowers. My favorite flowers actually," she said, giving them a fond look that for some reason had Dragon scowling.

"Aren't they like weeds?"

She shook her head in obvious disdain for his floral ignorance. "They aren't weeds. They're associated with love and passion. They're strong and brilliant and fruitful—their seeds feed everything from birds to people."

"So, you'd say they're a good omen, too."

"I would," she said.

"And on that second good omen, let's leave. We're too exposed out here, and it is almost dawn."

She nodded and, still sipping the wine, the two of them

left the meadow. Bryan carried her basket in one hand and held his sword in the other.

"Thank you for believing me," she said after they'd walked in companionable silence for a little while.

"You are welcome," he said.

She glanced at him. "You're not what I expected."

He met her gaze and smiled. "I'm shorter, right?"

Anastasia smiled back at him. "Yes. You're definitely shorter."

After a few moments Bryan asked, "Do you like shorter?"

She just kept smiling.

"I think you don't dislike me," he said.

She raised a brow at him. "I already told you that."

"Yes, but the spell proved it."

"And how did it do that?" she said.

"It's supposed to reveal the truth of me, and all of my," he paused, thinking, then continued, "and all of my arrogant misdeeds."

She felt her face get warm and she looked away from him.

"So, if I was really like that—all arrogant and full of myself and not caring about others—you'd see the truth of that and you'd dislike me."

She did look at him then. "No, you're wrong. Just because the truth of you is revealed, it doesn't mean the person seeing it will automatically dislike you—even if you are arrogant and full of yourself."

He laughed. "I think what you just said was nice, even though it didn't sound like it."

"And I think you're better at spells and rituals than you let on," she countered with.

"I think you'll have to look up my records to see."

"I'll do that," she said.

"You might be surprised by what you find," he said.

She met his gaze. "Yes. I might be."

The sun was just beginning to lift through the bluffs in the east when they reached the door that led to the professors' quarters in the main house. Bryan handed her the basket.

"Thank you," she said. "I–well–I suppose I will see you in class."

"Not this semester. I took Spells and Rituals last semester. But you will see me."

Anastasia drew a long breath and then said, "Dragon, about the kiss–"

He held up a hand to stop her words. "No," he said quickly. "Do *not* tell me it was a mistake."

"You're a fledgling. I'm a professor."

"Is that it? Is that the only problem you have with me?"

"That's enough," she said firmly.

Instead of being dissuaded, she watched a long, slow, triumphant smile tilt his lips. "Good, because that is only a temporary problem." He took her hand, lifted it, and kissed her palm. Then, still smiling, he fisted a hand over his heart and with perfect respect bowed to her and said, "Merry meet, merry part, and merry meet again, *Professor* Anastasia."

Before she could respond, he smacked her cheek with a quick kiss, turned, and strode away, whistling happily.

Dragon had been right—she was surprised when she looked up his records. "He's practically a perfect student," she muttered to herself as she thumbed through the files. She was also surprised by how the fledglings treated him, especially the ones who had come to her for love spells.

They didn't dislike him.

Granted, none of them hung on him or fawned over him

or flirted overtly with him. Well, none of the fledglings who had come to her for love spells flirted overtly with him. Others . . . yes.

Anastasia tried not to notice or care.

She couldn't help noticing, though, that in general the fledglings looked up to him. He was popular with everyone, and that included his professors. And Dragon, in turn, was charming and arrogant, witty and mischievous. And kind.

He was kind.

Anastasia couldn't even try not to care about that.

Whenever their paths crossed during the next several days, which they did frequently, his eyes found hers. His gaze lingered on her. Her gaze lingered on him.

And every morning she found a fresh sunflower in a crystal vase on her desk.

Anastasia was certain the entire House of Night would be commenting on the looks that passed between its newest Sword Master and its youngest professor. But it turned out they were completely distracted by a horrible human named Jesse Biddle.

"It's as if he's goading us," Diana was saying as the Tower Hill Council Meeting convened in the drawing room of the professors' quarters.

Anastasia, still feeling nervous about attending a Council Meeting, hastily took her seat and tried not to look surprised when Shaw, Leader of the school's Sons of Erebus

Warriors, entered the room followed by two of his most senior vampyres, as well as Dragon Lankford.

His eyes met hers for a heartbeat and he nodded briefly, before bowing and saluting the High Priestess.

"Good, everyone is here," Pandeia said. "The Council Meeting can now formally begin." She turned her attention to Shaw. "Explain exactly what took place last night."

"It was just after midnight. The Dark Daughters had gone to Bloody Island to perform the Fautor per Fortuna Ritual for the Sixth Formers. As they were asking Nyx to bless them and help them to be favored by fate with the Change, Biddle stepped out of the shadows, knocking over the ritual candles and breaking the circle," Shaw said, shaking his head with disgust. "The human forced them off the island. The High Priestess in Training said his gaze lingered hot and heavy on each of the girls, so much so that they felt tainted by it even after returning to their rooms."

"She told me she believes him to be quite mad," Diana said.

Pandeia spoke firmly, "I visited them today and I can tell you that I felt the echoes of fear and something dark and heavy lingering on them." The High Priestess addressed Anastasia: "Did you smudge them?"

"I did, and almost immediately each of them reported feeling better—*lighter* was the word they used," Anastasia said.

Diana's gaze speared Shaw. "And why was there no Warrior present to protect our young fledglings?"

"The Dark Daughters decided the blessing would be their gift to the sixth-former male fledglings, so there were no males, fledgling or vampyre, present. You know that quite often the Dark Daughters perform rituals separate from the Dark Sons," Shaw said, and Anastasia could see that he was trying to control his frustration. "That is why I have included Dragon Lankford at this Council Meeting. I propose that from now on, even if the ritual specifies only females be involved, male fledglings be present, if outside the circle."

"Is that enough protection?" asked Lavinia, the literature professor. "Should our vampyre Warriors not protect our fledglings? Perhaps they should accompany them whenever they leave campus."

Diana snorted in disgust. "Yes, if we want them to live as if they are prisoners. Our fledglings, especially our female fledglings, need to have the freedom to come and go as they please without an armed guard."

Pandeia sighed. "Perhaps the Dark Daughters should be directed not to hold rituals on Bloody Island until this conflict with the sheriff dies down."

"The island is ours!" Diana said, slamming her hand down on the table. "It has been named thus because of our rituals— we shouldn't allow an overbearing human to infringe upon the rights of our fledglings."

"St. Louis is no longer a barbaric outpost." Pandeia's answer was swift. "Its human population has more than doubled in the past few years. It has changed from a dusty trading post on the river to a thriving city."

"And Tower Grove was a thing of beauty and serenity when St. Louis was a filthy, uncivilized infant of a settlement," Diana said.

"Of course it was. Vampyres have always created beauty wherever we live. But with the changing times we cannot afford to alienate those who surround us, and if that means our Dark Daughters perform their rituals here on the vast acreage of Tower Grove and the prairie that we call home, rather than a sandy island within view of the city docks, then so be it. I hate to say it, but I can foresee a time when we will have to hide our identity from the human populace. It is a horrible thing to imagine, but a small price to pay for our young to be left in peace."

"Humans will never leave us in peace. They hate us!" Diana snapped.

"Not all of them," Pandeia countered. "Many of them do envy and fear us, but some of them respect us. You know there is no shortage of humans who willingly share their blood with us—there are even several vampyres here at this very Council Meeting who have human consorts, though the current trend is for humans to pretend disinterest in mingling with us."

"I am afraid, High Priestess, that the trend is more than simple disinterest. With Sheriff Biddle's encouragement, humans may think they can act against us," Shaw said.

"They cannot stand against our Warriors," Pandeia said, clearly upset at the direction the conversation had taken.

"Then let us send our Warriors into town to teach Biddle that he cannot harass our fledglings!" Diana said.

Anastasia couldn't stay silent any longer. "But, has the High Council not expressly forbidden Warriors to take action against humans other than in defense?"

Diana snorted. "That is a rule created by a Council who live in Venice—a place where it is considered *elegante* to be a human desired by a vampyre. They cannot comprehend what is happening here in uncivilized America."

"Enough!" Pandeia's voice had utterly changed, and the power of her command had the fine hairs rising on Anastasia's forearms. "Diana, your words are inappropriate. My House of Night will not rebel against its High Council. And one misguided human will not turn an entire city against us. We should remember that we were all once human."

Diana bowed her head. "Forgive me. I did not mean disrespect. It is just unthinkable that our fledglings should be afraid to leave campus unless they are disguised or in the company of Warriors."

"Which is why I agree with Shaw's inclusion of our newest Sword Master in this Council Meeting," Pandeia said.

"Dragon, I would like you and the sixth-former males who have shown Warrior aptitude to be sure that our females do not leave campus without at least one of you present in each group."

"Of course, High Priestess," Dragon said, fisting his hand over his heart and bowing his head to Pandeia.

"I know it is not a perfect solution to this problem, but it will ensure our girls are not so easily intimidated by Biddle, who, like most bullies, will probably lose interest in harassment when faced with more than young girls armed with candles and herbs. So they will be protected, and still have the freedom to come and go without being under a guard of adults." Pandeia looked at the rest of the Council Members. "I am going to send a missive to Venice. The High Council should be made aware of what has been happening here." Then she surprised Anastasia by saying, "Professor Anastasia, I have been impressed by the strength of your spellwork. I would ask that you cast a spell for the House of Night—something protective."

Anastasia hesitated and almost didn't speak except to agree placidly, but her mentor's firm voice spoke through her conscience: *Follow your instinct; trust yourself.* So she squared her shoulders and said what she felt she must. "High Priestess, I would respectfully like to recommend a different type of a spell."

"Other than one of protection? Why?"

Anastasia drew a deep breath and followed what her instincts were telling her. "A protective spell is, at its very heart, focused on violence. After all, if there was no need to protect against an aggressive act, the spell would not need to be cast at all."

"And is there something wrong with that?" Pandeia asked.

"Usually, no," Anastasia explained. "But in this case I wonder whether the very act of the casting wouldn't be like poking or prodding this Biddle person."

"I think poking and prodding him sounds like an excellent idea," Diana said, and several of the Council Members nodded agreement.

"Not if the goal is to have him leave us alone," Anastasia said. "That might actually keep us in his mind, when otherwise, with the presence of Dragon and the other Warriors in Training, Biddle would, as our High Priestess said, lose interest in us."

"You make a good point," Pandeia said. "What would you suggest instead?"

"A peace spell. And I wouldn't cast it here on our land. Even though recent acts have aroused our anger, we have peaceful intent. It is the human who needs spellwork. It would work best if I am closer to wherever Biddle finds sanctuary."

"The jailhouse near the town green. That is definitely his sanctuary," Shaw said.

"Then I should cast the peace spell near the jailhouse. As a side benefit it would have a general calming effect on the city, which would help soothe any human nerves Biddle has begun to fray."

"I have to agree with Anastasia. Cast your spell, Professor. Just be certain you are escorted by a Son of Erebus Warrior."

"It would be my honor, Professor," Shaw said, bowing to her.

"I do not mean to insult you, but I cannot cast a peace spell while I'm being guarded by a Warrior. It simply goes against the very heart of the spell."

"But it is not safe for you to go so near to Biddle's haven alone," Pandeia said.

"Is it just the presence of a vampyre Warrior that will disrupt the spell?" Diana asked.

"Yes."

Diana smiled. "Well, then, we will send the next best thing to protect you—Dragon Lankford. He is not yet Changed, so you will not be protected by a *Warrior,* though you will be watched over by a Sword Master."

"Would that not solve the problem of your protection?" Pandeia said.

Anastasia cleared her throat before she spoke. "Yes, it would."

The High Priestess turned to the young Sword Master. "What say you, Dragon?"

He smiled, fisted his hand over his heart, and bowed to Anastasia. "I say I am Professor Anastasia's to command."

"Excellent! Cast the spell tonight, Anastasia. St. Louis needs all the peace it can get as soon as possible," Pandeia said. "And this Council Meeting is adjourned. Blessed be to you all."

CHAPTER SEVEN

"You have been frowning since we left the House of Night," Bryan said, and then clucked to the pair of matched grays that were pulling the buggy. "Hey there, easy!" he soothed, glancing sideways at Anastasia. "See, even the horses can feel your frown."

"I am not frowning. I'm concentrating," she said, frowning. "But you're right about the horses acting skittish."

He grinned at her. "I'm right about more things than horse behavior."

Anastasia turned her body so she could look directly at him. "Has anyone ever explained to you the difference between confidence and arrogance?"

"If I say no are you going to lecture me?"

She hesitated before speaking and then said, "No, I don't think I will."

They rode on in silence and after a short time Dragon sighed. "Okay, lecture me. I like it. Really."

Anastasia opened her mouth to tell him that she didn't give a hoot about what he liked or disliked, but first he added, "Truth be told, I'd listen to you say anything. Your voice is pretty." His eyes met hers briefly. "Almost as pretty as you."

He sounded young and silly, but when she looked into his eyes she saw a depth of kindness that had her cheeks warming. "Oh, well, thank you. And thank you for the sunflowers, too. I'm assuming you're the one who has been leaving them for me," she said, looking quickly away.

"I am, and you are welcome. Did you like them? Really?"

"Yes. Really," she said, still looking away from him. Flustered at her own reaction, she tried to figure out if it was *this* Dragon she was responding to or the older version who still haunted her thoughts.

There was another long, silent stretch between them, and then he blurted, "They don't hate me."

Anastasia raised her brows. "They?"

"The thirteen girls and two boys."

"Oh, *they*. And how do you know that? I didn't tell you who *they* were."

He smiled. "Doesn't matter. No one's been hating me. You know what that means?"

"My spell didn't work?" she said, adding a smile so he knew she was kidding.

Dragon laughed. "You know *our* spell worked just fine. It means I'm not so bad."

"I never said you were."

"No, you said I'm an arrogant misdeeder."

"I don't think *misdeeder* is a word," she said.

"I just made it up," he said. "I'm good with words."

She rolled her eyes and muttered, "Boasting. Again."

He laughed again. "You looked up my records, didn't you?"

"Maybe."

"You did. And you found out I'm almost as talented at schoolwork as I am at sword work."

"Arrogant . . ." She breathed a long sigh and looked away from him so he couldn't see her smile.

"How is it arrogant if it's the truth?"

"It's arrogant if you boast, whether it's the truth or not," she said.

"Sometimes a vampyre has to do some boasting to get a priestess to notice him," he said.

Still not looking at him, Anastasia gave a little snort. "You aren't a vampyre."

"Not yet I'm not."

"And you have lots of females who notice you."

"I don't want lots of females," he said, all teasing gone from his voice. "I want you."

She did look at him then. His brown eyes were honest

and unwavering. This night his hair wasn't tied back and it framed his face, making his firm jaw seem more pronounced. He was dressed in a simple, unadorned black shirt and pants. She knew the color was supposed to blend with the darkness around them, but to her it made him look older, stronger, and as mysterious as the limitless night.

"I wish you'd say something," he said.

Her gaze went from his broad chest quickly up to his eyes. "I–I'm not sure what to say."

"You could tell me I have a chance with you."

"Am I just a conquest? Something for you to win, like the title of Sword Master?"

He pulled the buggy up short and turned to face Anastasia. "That's a load of bullocks! Why would you say that?"

"You're competitive," she countered. "You have a predator's skills. You chase. You catch. You conquer. I'm probably the only female in quite some time who hasn't fallen at your feet to worship you. So you want me because I'm a challenge."

"I want you because you're beautiful and smart, and beautiful and talented, and beautiful and kindhearted. Or at least I thought you were kindhearted." He blew out a long, frustrated breath. "Anastasia, the spell we cast was supposed to draw the truth about me. So, I'll admit to being arrogant." He shrugged. "I think with my skills a bit of arrogance is warranted. But I want you to understand that me wanting you has nothing to do with conquest or predatory skills."

His brown eyes captured hers and she saw hurt, not anger, in their depths. Slowly, she reached across the space between them and touched his arm. "You're right. You don't deserve that from me. I'm sorry. Bryan." She sighed and shook her head, correcting herself, "I mean Dragon. I'm a little confused about what I feel for you."

He covered her hand with his. "You can call me Bryan. I like it when you say my name."

"Bryan," she said softly, and felt him tremble under her hand. "I didn't expect someone like you in my life."

"It's because I'm a Sword Master, and going to be a Warrior, isn't it?"

She nodded silently.

"Why does that bother you?"

"You're going to think it's foolish," she said.

He took her hand from his arm and laced his fingers with hers. "No, I won't. I give you my promise. Tell me."

"I was raised a Quaker. Do you know what that means?"

"Not really. I've heard of them. Aren't they religious fanatics?"

"Some are. My family wasn't as bad as the rest of our community. They—they loved me," she said hesitantly, remembering. "Even though the community made them shun me after I was Marked and then Changed. But I still get letters from my mother. She sends them secretly. She still loves me. I know I'll always love her."

"That doesn't seem foolish. That seems loyal and faithful and kind," he said.

She smiled. "That's not the foolish part. What's foolish is that there are still pieces of me that are very much Quaker. I don't think that will ever change."

"You mean you don't worship Nyx?"

"No, Nyx is my Goddess. For as long as I can remember I've felt connected to the earth in a special way, a *different* way than my family. I think that's how I found my path to the Goddess, though my love of the earth." Anastasia brushed the hair back from her face and continued, "What I'm trying to tell you is that when I was human I was a pacifist. I'm *still* a pacifist. I think I always will be."

She saw him blink in surprise, but he didn't release her hand. "I can't change the fact that I'm a Sword Master. And I wouldn't if I could."

"I know! I don't mean–"

"Wait, I want to finish. I don't think me being a Sword Master and you being a pacifist is a bad thing."

"Even when I tell you I think mercy is stronger than your sword?"

"So is love. So is hate. There are lots of things stronger than my sword."

"I don't like violence, Bryan."

"You think I do?" He shook his head and answered himself before she could. "I don't! The reason I first picked up a sword was because I hate violence." His shoulders slumped and he continued with an honesty so raw it was almost painful to hear. "I'm short. I used to be *very* short. Little, actually. So little I got picked on. I was the butt of jokes. I was 'the Earl's middle son who was wee and soft and blond like a lass.'" He swallowed hard. "I didn't like to fight. I didn't want to fight. But that didn't matter. The violence came to me whether I wanted it or not. If I'd given up, given in to it—to them—I would have been broken and hurt and abused. You see, my father was not well liked, and his smallest son was thought to be his weakest link." He paused and Anastasia could see it was hard for him to talk about this part of his past—hard for him to go back there. "Instead of being broken, I grew strong. I learned how to use a sword to *stop* the violence done against me. Yes, I was good at it. Yes, I got arrogant and have probably used my sword when I didn't have to, especially before I was Marked. But the truth is that I prefer to stop violence rather than start it." His sword-roughened palm was calloused and hard against her smoother one, and she felt that rough touch all through her body. "A Warrior is a protector, not a predator."

"You live by violence," she said, but even to her own ears her words sounded weak. "You become something else when you fight. You've said it; others have said it. You're even named after it."

"I am a dragon only when I have to be and I will always protect my own," he said. "Try to believe that. Try to believe in me. Give us a chance, Anastasia."

Her stomach butterflied as she recognized his words. The older version of him, that vampyre Warrior she'd known she could love, had said the very same thing to her—and he had called her "my own."

"I will give us a chance," she said slowly, "if you promise to remember that mercy is stronger than your sword."

"I promise," he said.

And then Anastasia surprised herself by leaning forward and kissing him on his lips. When she and Bryan parted they looked into each other's eyes for a very long time, until he said, "After you cast the spell tonight, would you walk with me by the river, back to the meadow?"

"If you'll protect me," she said softly.

"I'll always protect my own," he repeated. Smiling, he tucked her arm through his and then clucked for the horses to get up and go.

Her arm was still tucked into his as they walked along the cobblestone-lined levee. Anastasia would usually have gazed at the steamboats, which were lined up, one after another, stretching all the way up and down this part of the river. As with some of the luxuries found at the House of Night, she wondered if she'd ever get used to the majesty of the steam-engine boats. They were such a drastic contrast to the city, which was dark and quiet at this late hour. The steamboats truly were floating palaces, still humming with activity, their gay chandeliers glowing, sounds of dancing girls and gamblers drifting over the water like magickal music. Usually her attention would have been occupied with peeking inside the mullioned windows.

But tonight Anastasia barely gave them a glance. Tonight she was completely distracted, and it wasn't rehearsing the up-coming spell that was the problem. The peace spell was actually one of the simplest to cast. There were only two ingredients, lavender for calming, which would be muddled into a cup for burning by Anastasia's favorite stone, an ajoite, the stone that had a turquoise phantom within its crystal depths and was always a conduit to peace and pure, loving energy. The spell was elementary: she muddled the lavender with the ajoite and then burned it over an earth candle as she spoke the ageless words of peace. It was easy, fast, and effective.

Then why did she feel so uneasy?

In the distance, over the sounds of revelry from the steamboats, she heard the distinct croaking call of a raven. Anastasia shivered.

"Are you cold?" Bryan pulled her closer to him. "Are you certain you don't want me to carry your spellwork basket? I have before," he said, smiling at her.

"I'm fine. And I have to carry the spellwork basket until after I cast the spell. I need to infuse it with my energy." She smiled at him. "You can carry it back to the buggy."

"Gladly," he said.

They walked on, and Anastasia suddenly stopped, pulling him to a halt beside her. "No, that's not entirely true. I'm not fine, and since you're my protector, I should be honest with you. Something is wrong. I feel uneasy—afraid."

He covered her hand with his. "You need not be afraid. I promise you that I am more than a match for any bullying human sheriff." Bryan looked into her eyes. "Bullies haven't threatened me for a very long time."

"Is that confidence or arrogance speaking?"

"Both." He smiled. "Come, let's finish this so we can move on to better things tonight." He pointed to a small park-like area just ahead of them and to their left. "The jailhouse is the square stone building on the other side of the town green."

"Good, yes, let's do get this done." Anastasia hurried forward with Bryan, ignoring the dark feeling that had been shadowing her since the Council Meeting. *It's nerves, that's all,* she told herself. *My House of Night is counting on me, and I'm being wooed by a charming fledgling. I just need to focus, ground myself, and do what I know I must.*

"What is it you need me to do?" Bryan asked as they walked through the little park and approached the dour stone building.

"Actually, the less you do the better." He looked at her quizzically and she explained. "Bryan, I know you're here as my protector, but that doesn't change the fact that you're a swordsman. You represent the opposite of a peace spell."

"But I–," he began, but she stopped him. "Oh, I know your intention is good, peaceful even, but that doesn't change your essence, your aura. It's that of a Warrior."

He grinned. She frowned.

"I didn't mean that as a compliment," she said, ignoring

his grin. Then she studied the stone building as she reasoned through the steps of the spell aloud. "I'm going to place the candles and cast the circle around the jailhouse itself. The front faces the river, which means it faces east. That's good. I would usually burn the lavender over the earth candle because I feel most closely allied to earth, but I want this spell to be carried throughout the city, so I'd already decided to use the air candle this time as a catalyst for the spell. I like that the entrance faces air in the east—it's a good omen," she said brightly, trying to ignore the nagging feeling of unease that simply would not leave her be.

"That sounds good—logical," he said, nodding. "So, I'll walk with you, but stay outside the circle?"

"No," she said, already prodding around in her basket, being sure the small, brightly colored tea light candles she'd brought were in order. "Just stay here in the park."

"But I won't be able to see you when you're on the rear and far sides of the building."

"No, but you'll be able to hear me," she said absently, already beginning to ground herself and focus on the spell at hand.

"Anastasia, I don't like that you're going to be out of my sight."

She glanced at him. "Bryan, this is a *peace* spell. From the moment I begin crushing the lavender, peace and calm will soothe from me. I know you're here to look out for trouble, and I'm glad you are, but the truth is, it is very rare, almost unheard of, for a priestess to be attacked during the casting of a spell such as this." Anastasia knew the words she was saying were true, but they felt wrong, as if some outside presence was weighing them and finding them lacking. She shook her head, more at herself than at Bryan. "No, you cannot follow me during the spell."

"All right. I understand. I don't like it, but I'll stay here." He pointed to a shadowy area at the edge of the park, well outside the meager gaslight illumination of the front of the jailhouse. "You know there is very little light around the building."

She raised her brows at him, "Bryan, I'm a vampyre. I only need very little light, and it's a good thing it's so dark here. It'll keep my spellwork from human eyes, remember?"

"I didn't mean–I'm just saying that–," he started twice, and then sighed, walked over to the area he'd pointed to, and said firmly, "I'll be here. Waiting for you."

"Good," she said. "This shouldn't take long, but I do tend to get caught up in my spellwork." Anastasia walked past him purposefully, giving his arm an absent pat.

"I know," he muttered, and then called to her, "You wouldn't even notice a rampaging bear."

"It wasn't rampaging," she called back, laughing.

He'd lightened her mood a little, so that she whispered

Nyx's name with a smile on her lips and, feeling more confident and serene, Anastasia placed the first candle—yellow, in the east for air—and called the element to her circle. Concentrating completely on the spell to come, she reached into the velvet bag that held the binding salt, and as she moved clockwise around the jailhouse, inviting the elements to create a circle, she sprinkled the salt in an unbroken line over the well-trod ground, whispering:

"Salt I use this spell to bind,
to seal intent, peace on my mind."

Foreboding pushed aside, Anastasia moved around the jailhouse, casting her circle and thinking calm, serene, happy thoughts. And, though she had decided to set the spell with the air candle, as she worked she automatically visualized reaching down deep into the soil below her and pulling up rich earth magick to help ground the spell and reinforce her intent.

As it had been doing since she'd attempted her first fledgling spell, the element responded to Anastasia, and strong, steady earth magick awakened beneath the jailhouse and began to flow.

The creature of Darkness and spirit that crouched in the basement felt the earth surge in answer to the gentle request of the young priestess, and it knew the time had come to do its master's will. It began a whisper of quite a different sort.

The human, who had taken to pacing back and forth, back and forth before the silver cage long into the night, paused and listened.

*"For the cold fire to survive
the vampyre Anastasia must not be alive."*

"Yes! Yes, I know." Biddle snarled the words at the creature. Compulsively, his head twitched and he kept plucking at his shirt, as if to rid himself of imagined insects that crawled over his skin. "But I can't get to her in the middle of that vampyre nest."

"Tonight she is near.
Kill her above, then bring her here."

"You mean she's outside? Alone?" Biddle didn't seem to notice that the creature's voice had changed, gone from a halting serpentine whisper that was barely human to a deep melodic chant that was far too seductive to be human.

"Her protector is Dragon Lankford,
but cold fire can conquer his sword."

From inside the cage the shadowy creature opened its maw wide and, with a terrible retching sound, sticky threads of blackness spewed forth from it, slithering to Biddle, who came forward eagerly to meet them. As if greeting a lover, he moaned in pleasure as Darkness wrapped around his legs and seeped beneath his skin, filling him with a power that was as addictive as it was destructive.

Swollen with borrowed might, Biddle pulled out the long knife he'd taken to carrying since he'd caught the creature—since he'd been feeding it blood.

"After the vampyre's blood feeds me,
more power for you there will be."

"Yes! With more power I can get rid of those goddamned vampyres forever! I'll pick 'em off one by one if I got to. And I'll start tonight with that arrogant little bastard." Biddle began up the narrow stairwell. Behind him the creature was still speaking:

"Do not get distracted by the boy!
With Anastasia gone he is but fate's toy."

Biddle plucked at his shirt, laughed to himself, and ignored the creature's words.

"Deep peace of the gentle breeze to you . . ."

Anastasia's spell drifted through the night to Dragon. He could see her silhouette in front of the jailhouse, just outside the edge of the flickering gaslights that framed the stone doorway. She spoke in the same singsong cadence she'd used for her drawing spell.

"Deep peace of the warmest fire to you . . ."

Dragon thought her voice was probably the loveliest sound he'd ever heard. It soothed him and made everything feel right in his world.

"Deep peace of the crystal seas to you . . ."

He had been worrying about the fact that Anastasia didn't like it that he was going to be a Warrior, but as she cast her spell, speaking the words and feeding the ajoite-crushed lavender to the fire, Bryan realized he didn't have anything to be troubled about.

"Deep peace of the timeless earth to you . . ."

It would be easy to convince Anastasia he wasn't really violent. He wasn't like he used to be. He was older and wiser. He only used his sword when he had to—or mostly only used it then. She would see.

"Deep peace of the shining moon to you . . ."

She would understand. Dragon let out a low, slow sigh and leaned more comfortably against the big oak. He was looking up at the sky and thinking that he'd been really smart to leave those sunflowers for Anastasia every day when it happened. One moment he was standing there, peaceful, filled with true contentment, and the next Biddle was in front of him.

Dragon stared at the man, frozen by surprise. In just the

few days since Dragon had last seen him, Biddle has gone through a terrible transformation. His face was gaunt. His cheeks, hollow. The skin under his eyes was puffy and dark. He twitched spasmodically. *This* was what had broken up the Dark Daughters' Ritual and run them off their island? Dragon thought he could snap the skinny human with one hand. He was obviously nothing but the pathetic shell of a man.

Dragon tried to keep the disgust from his voice when he said, "Sheriff Biddle, is there something I can do for you?"

Biddle smiled. "Yep. You can die."

For the first time in his life, Bryan Dragon Lankford looked into the face of true evil.

Instinct had Dragon reaching down to unsheathe his sword, but he was too late. Biddle struck with a speed and strength that was inhuman. He grabbed Dragon by the throat and rammed him against the hard bark of the oak tree, forcing the air to whoosh from his body. With his other hand the sheriff knocked the sword from Dragon's failing grip.

Biddle sneered into Dragon's face, saying, "You blustering little braggart!"

"No!" Dragon choked, trying to struggle for air. The eerie familiarity of the sheriff's words and actions shocked him to his core, and suddenly he was back in that stable four years before, losing his home and his family and his birthright all over again.

"And you know what," Biddle said, pressing his mouth

close to Bryan's ear. "I ain't gonna kill her up here and take her down there. I'm gonna do what *I* want. I'll take her down there and kill her, but first I'm gonna to have me some fun with that pretty little vampyre cunny."

Dragon's throat was on fire, and as everything went dark for him he heard Anastasia, much too close, scream his name.

CHAPTER EIGHT

Anastasia knew something was wrong. She could feel it like the change that happens in the air before a thunderstorm breaks. She was calling on the deep peace of each of the five elements when the wrongness slicked through the night, shattering her concentration and breaking the casting of the spell.

Automatically, her gaze turned to Bryan, to see if he knew what it was—knew what they should do. Horrified, she looked in time to see the human move so quickly that her brain tried to deny her eyes. He picked up Bryan Lankford, *Dragon* Lankford, Sword Master of Vampyres, by his throat and held him against a tree, and then began choking the life from him.

She didn't hesitate. Anastasia ran straight at the man who was killing Bryan. Screaming his name, she hurled herself into the man, trying to get him to let Bryan loose.

He did let Bryan loose so that he could knock her to the ground. Head reeling, fighting to clear the specks of light from her eyes, Anastasia crawled over to Bryan, reaching for his hand.

"Bryan! Oh, goddess, no!" He was so still, and his throat looked wrong, like it had collapsed. He wasn't breathing. She could see he wasn't breathing at all.

"Leave him be," the human growled. He grabbed for her, but Anastasia scrambled around the tree, avoiding his praying mantis reach.

"Want to play you a little hide-and-seek, do ya?" The human chuckled. "Well, there ain't nothin' wrong with a little foreplay. Biddle is comin' to get ya . . ." And he started to stalk her around the tree.

Anastasia looked into the man's eyes and saw that the fledgling High Priestess in Training had been right. Biddle was utterly mad.

She knew she only had seconds, so instead of trying to avoid the creature called Biddle, she crouched, put one hand on the thick bark of the tree. The other she placed gently on Bryan's throat. Anastasia closed her eyes and thought of the earth below the tree—the rich, timeless, living strength that she believed with all her soul to be there. She envisioned it as a green fountain shooting up through the ground, to the tree's roots, into the tree itself, and from there flowing into her, through her, and into Bryan.

"Come to me strong, wonderful earth;
a healing intent is the magic I birth!"

Instantly, heat surged from the tree trunk, into her hand, though her body, and into Bryan's neck.

"Time for foreplay to be over. Let's us get to the good stuff. Come on. I never had me no vampyre," and so saying, Jesse Biddle reached down, took her ankle in a grip that was like a blacksmith's metal press. As if she weighed no more than a child's doll, he dragged her from Bryan and toward the dark rear entrance of the jailhouse. Anastasia watched to see if Bryan made any movement at all—even the smallest hint of breath lifting his chest again. She saw nothing but his crumpled, still form before Biddle tossed her inside the building and slammed the door shut behind them.

"Sssshe is not dead!"

Anastasia stared at the thing in the cage. It wasn't bird. It wasn't human. It didn't even appear *real*. Except for the glow of its scarlet eyes it seemed unsubstantial, ghostly—something made of nightmares and shadows.

"Not yet she ain't," Biddle said. "I'm gonna have me some fun before I drain her."

"Using her wassss not part of the plan," the creature hissed.

"There ain't no *plan*! There's just me feeding you her blood so's you'll give me more of what I want. What happens before to her don't matter."

Anastasia looked from the creature in the cage to the sheriff. "What is that thing?"

"Don't rightly know," Biddle said as his hand slid up from her ankle to her calf. "Just ignore it—it ain't real anyway."

From where he'd thrown her on the dirt floor Anastasia kicked out, trying to break away from him, but his rail-thin body was deceiving. The strength in his bony hands was incredible, and with a single pull on her leg he jerked her back to him.

"No! Leave me alone! Don't touch me!" She struggled against him.

"Aw, come on. Everybody knows about you vampyre women. Y'all have lots a men. So, don't act like you're some kinda virgin."

Cold fear filled Anastasia, freezing her. She stared at the human who loomed like an animated skeleton above her.

He smiled. "That's right. Just be still and it'll go easier fer you."

Keeping one hand clamped around her ankle, Biddle began unbuckling the belt to his pants with the other.

It was then Anastasia knew the truth—this human was going to rape and kill her.

Oh, Nyx! Please help me! I don't want to die like this, she prayed frantically.

Then, through the shock and chill in her blood, she felt the warmth of the ajoite crystal that she'd shoved in her pocket as her spell had been broken, and beside it was the heaviness of a velvet bag filled with salt crystals.

As Biddle reached into his pants, Anastasia reached into the pocket of her skirt. She scooped a handful of salt out of the velvet bag and threw it into the human's face.

Biddle cried out and jerked back, blinking hard and wiping his tearing eyes. "You bitch!" he yelled.

He'd given her all the time she needed. Anastasia scrambled backward as she lifted the bag of salt and the fist-sized ajoite, a crystal infused with phantom magick from deep within the earth. Since ancient times, priestesses had been using it to bring peace through clarity of spirit, and now Anastasia, a priestess dedicated to peace and the earth, reached deep within her spirit and connected with the element on which she crouched. With a single motion she whipped the open bag of salt around her so that it surrounded her with a crystal circle, saying:

"Binding salt, of you I ask,
link me to earth as your task."

Then, holding the ajoite like a dagger, she plunged it into the dirt, crying:

"Earth below, filled with might,
grant me protection this dark night!"

She felt the surge of power come from below, as if a dam had broken free. Like a thunderstorm on the prairie, green light sizzled all around her. Pressing her palms flat against the element that had just gifted her with an affinity, Anastasia was weeping tears of happiness and thanksgiving when Biddle tried to cross the circle of salt. He recoiled with a cry of pain just as the creature in the cage shrieked, *"No! The green light! It burnsss me!"*

"Shut up, you!" Biddle kicked the creature's cage and the thing of spirit quieted to a keening whimper. Then he began to circle the glowing shield. "What is this? What have you done, you damned witch?"

"I've called my element to protect me. You can't hurt me now." She lifted her chin and met his gaze. "I'm not a witch. I am a vampyre priestess with an earth affinity, and *you can't hurt me now!*" she repeated.

"It won't last! It won't last!" Biddle said, nervously plucking at his shirt. "When that light dies, so do you."

Anastasia shook her head. "You don't understand. The earth is protecting me. It's not going to die or fade or fail. And I'm going to sit right here and wait for my High Priestess to find me. I promise you, she will. The House of Night knows I'm here. They'll find me and Bryan." Her voice started to break, but she pulled more power from the earth below her and continued, "And then you'll answer for what you've done tonight." Her gaze went from him to the pathetically whimpering thing in the cage. "And you'll have to answer for whatever you've done to that poor creature, too."

"Don't nobody care about vampyres *or* ghost things," he said.

"That's not true," Anastasia said, and as she spoke she felt the rightness of her words. "There are good people in St. Louis. They trade with us. They even become our consorts. They won't like what you've done, what you've turned into, or what you've trapped down here."

He paused and she saw a flash of something that might have been a spark of sanity in his eyes. "You know I'm right," she said. "Just leave here. Go, before anyone else is hurt."

Anastasia saw understanding or even regret in his eyes, and then there was the awful wet, violent sound of a sword being plunged through a body. Biddle's eyes widened as he stared down at the blade that had suddenly gone through his back and sprouted out of the middle of his chest. With surprising gracefulness, the sheriff dropped to his knees and then lurched sideways in a growing puddle of blood as Bryan pulled his sword free of him.

The fledgling stood over Biddle, breathing hard, his throat no longer crushed but still cruelly bruised and battered. His lips were pulled back to expose his teeth in a feral snarl, and Anastasia saw that he was completely the dragon then. The sweet fledgling was gone, as was the kindhearted, handsome Warrior. As she watched him breathe in the heady scent of blood that lifted around them, she knew when he crouched beside Biddle that he was going to slash the human's throat and drain him as he died.

The sense of foreboding that had been shadowing Anastasia all that night flooded her, and she knew then that her intuition hadn't simply been warning her about Biddle's plans. There was more, much more to it than that. Reaching deep to pull more earth magic to her, the priestess whispered, *"With earth's might cut like a sword—reveal the truth of Bryan Dragon Lankford."*

With a green flash of light an image appeared before Anastasia. It was Bryan, a fully Changed vampyre. He was on a battlefield, and again, he was completely the dragon. She gasped as she saw who he was slaying: brother vampyres.

What you see
is what will be
if his strength is not tempered with mercy.

The words were in her mind, but they weren't her own and though she'd never heard the voice before, Anastasia knew the Goddess, Nyx, was speaking to her.

Anastasia also knew what she had to do.

Bryan had drained Biddle dry of blood and, swollen with power and victory and violence, he was descending upon the creature of spirit in the cage with his sword raised.

"Bryan, stop!" Anastasia cried as she stood and stepped out of the protective circle to stand between him and the thing in the cage.

"Step aside, Anastasia. I don't know what it is, but it was allied with Biddle. It must die."

She held her ground and said, "Bryan, it's in a cage. Biddle was keeping it prisoner."

"I don't care!" Bryan practically snarled at her, his breath smelling of blood and hate. "It needs to be killed!"

Anastasia repressed the shudder of fear she felt at the sight of the base, violent being he had become. *It is him. It is still Bryan,* she reminded herself. Moving slowly, she reached out to cover his bloody sword hand with her own. "You don't care about that creature, but do you care about me?" she asked softly.

He hesitated. Through his hand she felt the tension in him release just a little. "Yes," he said. "I care about you."

"Then listen to me. There has been enough killing tonight. I'm asking you to let mercy win. Be stronger than your sword. Become the Warrior I know is within you."

Their eyes met, held, and when he finally sighed and lowered his sword Anastasia saw her future, her Bryan, within them.

"Yes," he said, touching her cheek gently. "I choose to become the Warrior you believe is within me."

Anastasia was stepping into his open arms when his face twisted in pain and, with a terrible cry, Bryan fell to the ground at her feet.

Frantically, she dropped to her knees beside him. "Bryan! What has–"

And then she broke off as he raised his tear-streaked face to her.

"Oh!" She breathed a long, awestruck breath. "They are so beautiful." With a trembling hand, she reached out and traced the new tattoos of the fully Changed vampyre beside her.

"What are they? What do they look like?" he asked.

"Dragons," she said. "They look exactly like dragons."

"Dragons!" he said, laughing. And then almost immediately he sobered and took both of her hands in his. He cleared his throat and on his knees beside her said, "Anastasia, I want to be your Warrior. My lady, will you accept my pledge of my heart, body, and soul as your protector?"

"Only if you add one more pledge to that. Bryan Dragon Lankford, if you are pledged in service to me, you must give me your oath that from this moment on you will temper your strength with mercy."

With no hesitation he responded, "I do so pledge my oath to you." Bryan fisted one hand over his heart and bowed his head to his priestess.

He helped her to her feet and Anastasia's gaze went from him to the indistinct creature of spirit and darkness that crouched watching them from within silver bars of Biddle's cage. "Please, show mercy to it," she said simply.

"Then let my first act as your Warrior be a merciful one." He strode over to the cage. "Creature, I know not what you are, but I warn you, if you mean harm to us, I will protect my own."

"*Freedom . . . ,*" the thing said with its strange, whispery voice.

Holding his sword at ready, standing between the ghost thing and his priestess, Bryan reached down and opened the cage. There was a flapping sound, and then the creature faded completely away, hissing, *"It is finisssshed . . ."*

"Thank you, Bryan," Anastasia said.

Her Warrior took her in his arms, saying, "Come to me,

my lady, my own," and Anastasia happily and naïvely stepped into what she truly believed would be their happily ever after.

At the same moment in the bowels of the earth a winged prisoner stirred and through the scarlet eyes of the creature Dragon Lankford had just released, Kalona began to hunt for another piece of the puzzle that would align the fates and bring to fruition his desires for the future.

EPILOGUE

Present-day Oklahoma

"No!" Though tears tracked down his face, Dragon Lankford's voice was like stone as he stared into Jack's funeral pyre. "I can never forget or forgive. That thing I allowed to escape—it was the spirit of a Raven Mocker, the creature who, given a body, murdered you. Had I destroyed it all those years ago, my own, my love, we might have avoided this fate, this future." He shook his head and repeated, "No, I can never forget."

Then, with cold, perfectly controlled movements, Dragon fisted his hand around Anastasia's locket and pressed it over his heart, bowing his head and saying, "I no longer have a priestess. I no longer am bound to my oath. Without you, Anastasia, I am only the dragon, and a dragon does not temper strength with mercy." He opened his fist and held the locket up before him, kissed it, and then threw it into the burning pyre.

Green flames blazed from the pyre and reality divided

and opened, curtain-like, to reveal a ghostly vision of Anastasia. She was sobbing and her voice, echoing eerily, came to him.

"You have cut my heart with your sword,
Bryan Dragon Lankford."

He fell to his knees in despair, reaching toward the flames as if he could pull her spirit to him, and cried:

"Your death has broken me;
the dragon is all I have left to be."

The apparition was fading, but her voice drifted over the crackle of the fire:

"If you are not my mate, kind and true,
how will I ever again find you?"

As his hungry eyes stared at her, Anastasia, still weeping, turned from the rent in reality and stepped into the arms of Nyx. The Goddess pressed a palm to her forehead and light cascaded into the priestess's soul.

"Nyx!" Dragon cried. "Let her remain with me!"

The Goddess's gaze was infinitely sad.

"You must be brave
to find the peace that you crave."

The curtain to the Otherworld shivered and closed, cutting off Dragon's vision of his mate and the Goddess.

"Brave!" he shouted. "That is your only answer for me before you steal away my mate? How can you be so cruel? I deny you, Nyx! I found Anastasia once on my own. I'll do so again, but only after I have exacted revenge for her untimely death. *Thus I do swear on my sword—my oath as Dragon Lankford!"*

Dragon stalked away into the darkness, and the sickly white flanks of an enormous bull caught the reflection of the moon as the beast, pleased, turned away to pursue other pleasures.

In the Otherworld, Nyx gazed down at Anastasia's fallen Warrior and wept.

The End for Now
Stay tuned for more from Dragon in the next House of
Night novel
Destined
On sale in November 2011.